SHOOTING THE BRIDGE

A Story of 17th Century Intrigue

*This story originally appeared in
'Spikey and the Green Wasp'
by the same author*

*To Lita
xx Dave (Dan)*

Copyright © 2021 Dan Tunnelly

The Moral right of the author has been asserted.

All rights reserved.

Apart from any fair dealing for the purposes of research or private study, or criticism or review, as permitted under the Copyright, Designs and Patents Act 1988, this publication may only be reproduced, stored or transmitted, in any form or by any means, with the prior permission in writing of the author, or in the case of reprographic reproduction in accordance with the terms of licences issued by the Copyright Licensing Agency

-o-o-o-

The characters herein, other than the obvious figures, historical or contemporary, are the product of the author's imagination and any resemblance to real persons, living or dead, is purely coincidental.

SHOOTING THE BRIDGE

A Story of 17th Century Intrigue

Dan Tunnelly

Also by Dan Tunnelly
(all available on Amazon)

Jagga's Limelight
All the Stages are a World

When Jagga Finn invokes his long-standing love of theatre and embarks upon his own fantastical, theatrical journey, little does he realise that Mattie, his cherished partner in life, will be swept into that same world of pretence and confusion. Do we each seek and find our path in life or does our path seek and find each of us? Do we believe in what we make of life, or is it all make-believe? In truth, we shall never know...

-o-o-o-

Black Joke Omnibus
Hell's Bells Unleashed

A surreal story, set in the 1970s/80s, relating a blackly comedic murder and involving Morris men and a mad coach excursion, with hosts of other characters, into the English Cotswolds towns and countryside.

-o-o-o-

What in Blue Blazers?
A History in Education

Another surreal fiction, set in the 1950s and 60s, involving suspicions of riotous, destructive plots at Millstone Grammar interspersed with nostalgia for the preoccupations of youth.

-o-o-o-

Spikey and the Green Wasp
A Tale of Two Wheelers

Here's a quirky tale set variously in the 1960s, the 1670s and points in between. First and foremost it's a gentle 'road movie' involving Jack and the love of his life 'Spikey' journeying on the innocent adventures of youth through the oft-misrepresented realm of Mod-hood.

Along the way there's the rather odd world of Narky Dionysus and his bookshop with a dip into the pages of its dusty tomes and an excursion into the mysterious happenings around the Shooting of London Bridge *(now recounted herein)*.

-o-o-o-

Behind the Silvered Cobwebs
Reflections in the Flash of Time
(a collection of poems)

Many of the words herein were written in the guileless flush of youth in the nineteen sixties and seventies. A few are written more recently. Sadly, I did not date these offerings, so they are here presented simply in several broad categories. In revisiting these distant fragmentary expressions, peeking behind the silvered cobwebs, I can see that they are simply a collection of emotional thoughts thrown at the page, often reflecting a confused and an angst-ridden journey through youth's hopes and fears... and loves... and sometimes despairs. They are but raw reflections of formative times and are what they are.

-o-o-o-

Myre Hamlet
& the Ice Wolf

The rural idyll of Myre Hamlet is taken with ill fortune brought from a distant land and so ensues the doubtful quest to put things right.

When Seth Linden leads the men of the Hamlet on a journey to find the remedy for their afflictions, they are taken to the realms of doubt and despair. Along the way, they find companionship and aid in unexpected places, yet harrowing misfortunes and ill encounters with surreal and evil forces lead them to confront their hopes and fears, whilst Seth comes to ponder upon his own inner self.

-o-o-o-

Dedicated to all those
who may indulge
in time and tide

CONTENTS

1) Splash

2) Abaddon

3) A Fair Frost for a Frost Fair

4) Jebila

5) Botolph Wharf

6) Long Acre

7) Hawker's Moon

8) Gold for the Taking

9) Tower Wharf

10) A Goldsmith Too Far

1

Splash

Autumn 1676. He hears the splash… a brief punctuation in the quiet of the fog-filled late afternoon as he sits moored off Queenhythe Stairs upstream from London Bridge. A splash is nothing new to him, but this night it's followed by a half-submerged peruke floating by on the murky waters. More often it's a hat, but this looks like a *gent* has met his match in the river, by cruel chance or by evil design. No use calling for help from the constables… all's quiet again after the splash.

'The poor soul will doubtless be beyond the bridge and half way to Wapping by now,' he thinks.

As a waterman, Samuel Bridgewater spends most of his waking hours on the river. He's been on the Thames these past twenty years since he was a boy learning watercraft from his father. And like his father and grandfather before him, he plies his necessary trade, his oilskins protecting him from the wet and the wind in winter and in summer shedding his winter coat to take in the heat of the sun and to breathe in the benign breezes.

SHOOTING THE BRIDGE

But tonight he'd been in deep contemplation of his life in this rat-infested place, where the vibrant, 'respectable' face of commerce pays scant regard to the dank and dismal lifeblood of the city... the trade carried on the rolling river. His boy of fourteen, John, is absent tonight, struck by a fever, nursed by a kind neighbour. The boy's mother, Aggy, is absent every night, taken some ten years or more before by the pestilence that had plagued the existence of the Capital into near-submission.

There'd been little trade for Samuel on the water today and it's time he was home. In any case he'd intended to be back early for the sake of the boy's nurse. The reeking fog is everywhere about the city, meandering stealthily along the darkling streets, skulking in sad doorways and penetrating to the very core of all those foolish enough, or desperate enough, to be abroad. There's been precious little traffic on the river and it seems that everyone but Samuel has gone to ground already. Like the rats, they're secure in their holes at home, or else ensconced beneath the lighted tallows in their local drinking holes, safe from the fetid murk that creeps into every muscle, every bone and into the recesses of Samuel's mind. Here is the Thames, his daily companion, fathomed deep in the souls of ages past and present; from the Romans to the Saxons, the Normans to the Tudors, and now the Stuarts with their history of sad beheading, their restoration and the growing disappointments of their profligate dynasty. In spite of everything, the river flows on, bound up with the merchants, the builders, the sailors, the butchers and bakers, the weavers and tanners, the plagues and the fires. And through it all the insignificant folk, often overlooked by those who feed on them, battling for survival in the mad helter-skelter of activity, all too readily spiralling downwards to the river with a splash. The river, like a great wayward artery, carries the wealth of England pumping in and out of the city, drawing it in from or spewing it out to the sea, or else clotting it in the eddies and swirls, sometimes running it aground on the inner shores of the river's meandering path; the flotsam and jetsam of ages, the detritus of the human condition, the putrid waste from the tanneries, the dregs from the breweries, the shit from man and beast alike, and even their unfortunate bodies… the bodies of forlorn or abused souls.

Yet for all this sombre contemplation, Samuel is an optimistic creature. His boy will soon be up and about again, his dear departed wife is surely in God's heaven, and tomorrow the fog will lift to reveal a clear blue sky, the sun glinting on the pinnacles of the new buildings that had risen day by day in defiance of the Great Fire that had so cruelly taken much of the old. River customers will be out and about again. But for now: *'Time to be home,'* he thinks.

He hears the cough… a deep, assertive cough. And there on the wharf, back lit by a linkboy's lanthorn, stands a burly, unkempt figure of dubious intention. His tailcoat is heavy with years of wear and street-grime. His felt hat, shapeless as a puddle of porridge, has felt the years. He's held together with a broad leather belt and a buckle too large. His belly, large too, is fighting to be free of his coat. His grimy neckerchief, loose for want of retying betrays a

SHOOTING THE BRIDGE

tattoo upon the side of his neck, discreet of size, no bigger than a penny coin, yet disquieting... a snake's head with jaws wide and with venomous teeth sneering.

"I need a waterman to get me across the river."

"Sorry, friend. I've knocked off. This is not the weather for messing with Old Man Thames."

"Well I say otherwise, my friend... if my light is to be worth this 'ere candle, then I say I've got to you in time. I need to be in Bear Garden, over on the south bank."

"Look around you, if this devilish fog will allow. Anyone with sense has run to cover or else to drink. Don't you think you should do the same 'til morning?"

"Not a chance, my dear. The night demands I cover the ground before I drink. The south bank is necessary."

"But why not take the bridge? Far safer."

"You'll know as well as me, it's closed off for the night already. Now... quick-sharp, my friend."

The linkboy quakes, no more than thirteen if he's a day, thin in the flickering candlelight, still hoping for his coin, and the shimmering silhouette of this unwelcome character seems to grow larger, agitated, his shadow dancing here and there on the algae-ridden decking of the wharf to the tune of the candle. Samuel thinks better of confronting the fellow further and agrees to take his fare, despite the danger.

So, the boy is paid off and slips away with his faltering flame like a Will-o'-the-Wisp on a Fenland marsh. Samuel's *own* lanthorn is lit now.

'*At least the tide is right,*' he thinks. '*I can manage this flow. And thanks to the fog, there'll be no other fools out there to be a-hindering us. I'll be back to see my John in the wink of an eye.*'

Splash

"So why are you bound for Bear Garden? Not much doing there in this weather, I guess," he asks of his fare.

"Never you mind," snaps the unsavoury character. "My business is mine and yours is yours. Let's keep it that way."

"Then you won't mind me asking for coin before we set off," says Samuel.

"Here, take it," says the would-be passenger, holding out coins in a grubby hand.

The stranger's bite doesn't unnerve the boatman. He sees confrontation every day in one form or another… more so these past ten years. Whilst the plague of 1665 had brought compassion in some, it had seen Londoners at large turn their minds inwards and their anger outwards, more from the need for self-preservation than from malice. Then the fire had destroyed all hope for many. More livelihoods than lives were lost and despite the concerted rebuilding, or perhaps at times because of it, crime has flourished and grown. Theft and embezzlement, misogyny and rape, all manner of abuse and violence, assault and murder all play a grisly part in the resurgence of the city, and out of it all comes much domestic strife and despair. Nonetheless, the commercial activity in the area destroyed by the fire has brought prosperity to those who have taken a lead, but decadence flourishes and grows darkly without check in the Capital these days, not least south of the river.

"What's money, when you need your bed?" adds the uncouth brute as he steps aboard.

Samuel pockets the fare and pushing off from the quayside with a nifty oar, relocates it in its rowlock as the

SHOOTING THE BRIDGE

boat peeps out gingerly into the mainstream. For a moment, the flow catches the boat, briefly persuading it downstream but Samuel knows the waters well enough. He compensates, and soon they're headed for the nether bank. In the distance down river, through a swirling break in the fog, he sees warm tallows shining out from houses on the bridge, beaconing against foolhardy approaches, each pinpoint of light a halo in the mist. Like a myriad of distant lighthouses warning of rocks in the seas, they flag the rapids running treacherously through the buttressed bridge.

The lonely boat, mists curling around its prow, reaches the far bank. Woodcock Skeleton, for that is his name, clambers out awkwardly then takes flight without a word into the Southwark darkness with the merest rustle like autumn leaves, a fleeing spirit of the night, gone to who knows where.

"Well, thank you waterman, for your kind assistance," whispers Samuel to himself. And his thoughts turn homewards again. He's anxious to see how young John is faring. The nurse will be keen to get to her own home on this Godless night.

Regaining Queenhythe safely, Samuel stows his boat in the boatshed, climbs the stairs and makes his way across Thames Street and on to Garlick Hill, turning into the back-alley where is home, paying brief regard to the plague-masked and cloaked figure that scurries by in the opposite direction on the hill.

'All these years on and still the plague haunts our London,' ponders Samuel. *'Happen the poor wretch sees this miasma as the bearer of disease. What would dear Aggy think, I wonder?'*

Splash

"Well now, Goody Robson. How's the boy?" calls Samuel, as he negotiates the hallway of the humble back-street dwelling he calls home. "I'm sorry to keep you so late. I took a fare unlooked for, but the cash is always welcome you know."

"The boy's well enough, Master Sam. The fever seems to be abating, but he'll be abed yet awhile, I fear. His strength is drained from all the heaving and sweating but I'm sure he's over the worst. Starve a fever, feed a cold is what I say, but now he's on the right side of it he should be eating. I prepared him fish broth but he wouldn't take it... says it tastes damp, he does. Well now, I says to him... *you'd* taste damp if you'd been swimming in the river all your life."

"I'll have words with him. I'm sure your fish broth is delicious, Goody. I want him back between the oars, and he needs his belly filling for that."

"Very good, Master Sam. I'll serve up a portion for *you* before I leave for home, along with a cut of bread."

"Er... don't trouble, Goody. I'll help myself when you're gone and I'll try the boy with it again."

"Very good. There's plenty there for tomorrow morning too. And I can come again then if you wish it."

Samuel's place had been razed to the ground in the Great Fire and, when he'd been able to return, his landlord had raised the rent stingingly to help cover rebuilding costs, despite the place having been resurrected in the main with salvaged materials and put together like a pig-barn by the cheapest builders to be found. In any case, all the decent craftsmen had been commanding good wages from those who could, or would, afford a decent job.

"Well, I'm true-grateful for all your help, Goody. You get home now and I'll see you again tomorrow, if you're willing. The boy likes you, don't you John?"

"Yes, father. Goody is so thoughtful and kind."

" I think he sees in you the mother he never got to know, my dear."

"That's as may be, Samuel, but I'd rather he's soon well again so as not to need me."

"You know you're always welcome here, whether young Johnny is well or no. But if he's up by tomorrow night, I'll settle with you then. In the meantime, go with care tonight. There're some odd folk about. I took a sly character over the river to Bear Garden. That's why I'm late. Wouldn't say what his business was. He was a rogue up to no good if you ask me. Then on the way back here I saw a plague-runner, mask and all. He seemed to be fleeing from imagined shadows of the past, but then you can hardly blame a soul in these desperate times."

"I'll be alright, Master Sam. No one will trouble an old crone like me. And if they do, they'll get the sharp end of my tongue, or else this blade."

To Sam's surprise, she flashes a dagger as sharp and keen as the startling glint that flares in her eye.

"Then, I'll stay out of the alley while you're about, dearest Goody, for the love of my vital parts."

"Father," calls out Johnny. "Will you stay with me tonight? I'm a-feared with all this talk of rogues and daggers."

"Of course I shall, John. And either Goody or me will be at hand through tomorrow. Then, once you're well

Splash

recovered, it's down to the boats again with me. You've a lot to learn before you take out your own boat on the water. There's more to fear from the river than from any stranger unless you get to know its ways well. Old Man Thames bites more bleak than any man and he's more capricious than any woman. You mark my words... he's not to be played with, my lad."

"I'll be away then, Samuel," says Goody.

"Of course, Goody. Tomorrow at eight then?"

"Eight it is, Master Sam."

The door latch clicks behind her and Sam bolts it secure.

"Now then, young John. So you don't fancy a slurp of this here fish stew?"

"No father. It really *is* damp, and I saw a fish eye floating in it."

"Then how about a hot potato from the fire? I'll pour the broth into the gutter... the rats don't mind damp. But don't tell Goody. She'd be might upset. And while our supper's roasting, I'll tell you a tale of the river."

"Thank you father. I do love your stories."

"Well now, young John. You say you're a-feared of being alone. Now there's no need... for if you are truly alone, then there's no one there to harm you. The time to be afraid is when you're with someone... someone you can't be sure of, that is."

"I see. But how do I know if I can trust someone?"

Well, that's what you need to learn. There was a time, before the plague and the Great Fire, when *I* was only nine... they'd butchered King Charlie's father only a year before and Olly Cromwell was ruling the roost. Now, like many another, I'm no believer in anyone having a divine right to rule the people and so I felt the king needed bringing down a peg. But I reckon they should have left him with his head. After all, you can't do much without your head, can you, Johnny?"

"I suppose not, father."

"Well, this dark night, the Roundheads came a marching through the streets, as bold as brass, as if they owned all the world. They were looking for Royalist sympathisers and one among them was a right bugger of a brute, sword in hand and slashing sacks of grain for no apparent good reason. Then there was a gentler fellow who seemed less foul. He would stop to ask questions... 'Why this?' and 'When that?' And after they'd ransacked all around, they left as quick as they'd arrived. Next morning, they found a woman dead, slit from ear-to-ear, despoiled by one of the soldiers, so I heard your grandfather say."

"And was it the slasher that did it?"

"Well, there's the thing. It turned out that the quiet one was the villain of the piece. He'd had a hatred of women for many a year, always being disciplined for his wanton ways, so it seems he took it out on *her*. And the slasher... he'd been feigning wild... as a cover, following the quiet fellow's every move. And, by all accounts, the next thing he slashed wasn't a sack of grain... it was a sack of bile in the form of the quiet soldier. The army didn't punish him for it either. They were glad to get rid of the sneaky one. *He* was the one bringing them into disrepute and making it hard for them to gain the trust of anyone."

"So it's always the quiet ones is what you're saying father?"

Splash

"No, son. What I'm saying is that it's not always the noisy ones. You need to hold people at arm's length before you go assuming that you can trust them whether they seem fair or foul. Handsome is as handsome does in the end, lad. That's a lesson worth observing."

"I suppose so, father, but what of the river story you promised?"

"Of course, Johnny. I'll tell you now."

"Is it a true story?"

"As true as I sit here, my boy. You know, Old Man Thames has many a story to relate, but this one, or one much like it, has happened more than once, truth to tell. It's about shooting the bridge."

"Well what's the point of shooting a bridge? You can't kill a bridge, can you?"

"No, but this is a different kind of shooting. You've seen from time to time, when the boatmen take their boats through the arches between the buttresses… well that's called *shooting* the bridge.

"Well don't *you* do that, father?"

"I've done it a time or two, Johnny but it's not a wise thing to do, unless the tides and the water flow are at their best behaved. Most sane watermen avoid it. If they *do* decide to ply their trade both sides of the bridge, they're fussy in choosing when to and when not to shoot the bridge. And even if they do, customers themselves are usually reluctant. Fearful, they get put ashore at Swan Stairs and walk to the far flank of the bridge to re-join the boat or, if the water's wrong, they'll take another boat that's working on the east side."

"It sounds exciting, father."

SHOOTING THE BRIDGE

"Well, John, there was this fellow, a waterman, like your father."

"Like *both* of us, father."

"Well, yes. In good time you too. Anyway this waterman was a fine oarsman. Strong of arm and straight of back, he was. He could out-row anyone on the river, big or small, short or tall. Your grandfather told me that he knew him… even drank with him on occasion. Not only was he faster than any other, but he could row further by far. He'd shoot the bridge more than anyone, and risk the rapids at wrong tide too. He'd take on customers who demanded more than the everyday journey and would often row the four miles to Deptford and back. Once or twice he even went to Woolwich… a whole ten miles each way. People though him a bit mad you know, yet they showed him great respect. Then as he grew older, and wiser you would think, he felt it made more sense to take on a sailboat, so as to spare him from much hard effort."

"A sailboat like the ones on the river now?"

"Yes, though this was a tall one. And, when the wind was in the west, he could make it to Deptford in double quick time with half the labour. And on the way back, it was all the better too, for he was less tired and, if tacking against the wind proved impossible, he could row with fresh strength."

"Does anyone drown in the river when they shoot the bridge, father?"

"They do, lad. And that's what I'm coming to. Our boatman was determined to stay king of the river, forever trying to complete the journeys ever faster. Now one thing that slowed him down when sailing was the bridge. His sailboat had a tall mast… as tall as any you would see, except for the navy ships. But the arches of the bridge, as you know, are low when the tide is high… low enough to hinder *his* mast at any rate. And you yourself will have seen, the taller sailboats on the river now, those that *sail* to the east will moor up like I've said on the west side of the bridge, drop and stow their sail then drop the mast and row out through the rapids of the bridge arches. Then on the east side they'll moor again to raise the mast and the sail before they can be away. The rapids are fickle enough for rowboats, but *sailing* through is far more perilous and to be avoided."

"Of course, father. It's true. I have seen all the boatmen pushing and shoving their boats to find moorings by Swan Stairs."

"It's true indeed. And there came a day when one of our famous waterman's fares grew impatient of the crowds and, ignoring the safety of the stairs, the boatman took it upon himself to shoot the bridge on the fly… he sailed within a gnat's breadth of the arches and with great speed, dropped the sail and mast as if in one swift move, and taking up his oars guided the boat on the boiling waters between the buttresses, adding danger to danger in the shooting. His fare that time had been an irritable couple… a henpecked but spiteful-looking man accompanied by his dreadful nagging wife who huffed and puffed and badgered her husband to harass our hero to hurry them on their journey. But once they were out into the rolling river and the wife realized that she'd pestered her husband into persuading the boatman to

SHOOTING THE BRIDGE

such an unwise tactic, she screamed so loud in terror that even deaf folk in Southwark could hear her. And the boat was spat out like a gob of phlegm and onwards into calmer water on the far side."

"What awful people, father. If I'd been the boatman, I'd have made them wait like all the others on the river."

"Well, John. That's exactly the thing to do. You see, a week later, the same couple found themselves by chance in the same boat. This time they, especially the wife, seemed to be in less of a hurry, but *'I'll show 'em,'* thought the boatman. And he chose to shoot the bridge once more rather than mooring up as they asked. But on this day, the tide was all wrong and the rapids were more vengeful. As they approached he tried to drop the sail but the ropes were all tangled and he was caught in the swirling current, out of control. The boat turned side on to the bridge and toppled this way and that. The scold of a wife was tossed into the boiling waters and the mast, still erect, struck the bridge with a crack like the crack of doom and, for all his efforts to right the boat, the boatman and the hen-pecked husband were thrown against the piers."

"Oh, father. How awful. Did they survive?"

"Well, only if they swam ashore and stayed hidden from the world from that day on... for all that was found was the splintered mast and a few ropes all entangled in the bridge. Even the boat itself was lost to London... carried maybe to the sea along with the waterman and his passengers."

"So why do watermen still do it today, father? When it's so dangerous."

"It's odd indeed, though no one tries approaching the

bridge with their sails raised. And the splintered mast from that man's wrecked boat was set upon the wall at the north end of the bridge as a reminder against such folly… you'll see it there to this day if you look. But, you'll find as you grow that more than a few are so impulsive in many things, especially when money dictates to time. Remember, John. In all your days, go at your own pace. Do not be persuaded by others, or even by yourself, to rash actions."

"Of course father. I see the sense in that. Don't shoot the bridge if you want to live another day."

"That's right, my lad. Now let's get these potatoes eaten, and then to sleep with you. You'll feel much better on the morrow. Tomorrow *is* another day."

Next morning comes. The fog has fled as quickly as it had swept in across the city and church bells are calling their waking flocks to hear the gospels of hope and resurrection. Sam, unlike most, will be busy again on this Lord's Day. Many of the good folk are soon out and about to church or else hither and thither visiting friends and relatives in, for them, far-flung parishes. And the bad folk, the ne'er-do-wells, are out weaving their dark webs along the alleys and down at the hithes.

At the *Sign of the Watchmaker* in Little Trinity Lane, the street-clock is striking eight as Goody raps on Sam's door. He's already up and preparing for the day's business. Young John, after a restless night, has settled with the coming of daylight, but Sam is glad that Goody is here to stay with him today. She's flustered as she enters.

"Morning, Goody. What troubles you?"

SHOOTING THE BRIDGE

"Morning, Master Sam," she offers. "It's not me that's troubled, but my dear friend, Hann... Hannah Smithson... the goldsmith's wife. Up on Cornhill they are. Her husband, Zeke was left for dead last night by some evil fiend. And die he did. Throat slit before he retired to bed as he pondered on his stock... all for the want of a couple of gold coins, it seems. Hann is distraught. Zeke meant the world to her, even if he was in some ways bested by his obsession with gold. After all, that most noble of metals has given them a comfortable living if not a comfortable life. She sent her son, Talman to break the news to me. He seems to bear it bravely, but his little sister, Eliska will be devastated. The girl was the apple of her father's eye. She's but twelve years old, poor thing. As for Talman, he perhaps cares enough for his family but I hear he's never been keen to be part of the business. He has an associate who takes him often from the home these days and into the deep intrigues of the city. I hope that this awful affair brings him closer to home again."

"What in God's name is the world coming to, Goody? The wealth of others doesn't go down well with the poor, but it has to be admitted, that it trickles down to the rest of us, in course of time, and so is beneficial. Many of my best customers are rich after all and they can pay well, without hesitation. And how should we feed ourselves without them?"

"*You* certainly eat well enough, Master Sam, but only by your hard endeavours. The rich are fine by me as long as they've earned it. And by the way, talking of food, I'll try the lad with the fish broth again. I'm sure he'll acquire a taste for it."

Splash

"You're too late, Goody… I persuaded him last night and together we made an end of it. The boy is much better, though he's still abed," says Sam.

"I'll go and raise him now," says Goody. "Maybe he could take the air with me later this morning. So, the broth it went down well then?"

"Well… it went down," whispers Sam to himself as she makes to climb the stairs. "Goody," he calls after her. "You must go at once to see what you can do for Hann. I'm sure Johnny is well enough to be left today, thanks to your care."

"Nonsense, Master Sam. There's no need of that. Hann has Talman with her and her close neighbours are to hand. A constable is there now, looking to find out exactly how it all happened. It's best I stay away, for today at least. Oh dear, oh dear. Hezekiah was such a good man… always a ready smile and he did so much for the parish. But oh, what evils lurk in man's shadowy cupboard."

"Look, Goody. I'll be back early, so you can go to her before dusk if you wish it then on reflection. Poor woman. What has London come too?"

Within the week, with the sad formalities of preliminary investigations completed, yet with no clues as to the culprit's identity, Hezekiah is buried in the churchyard of the new St. Michael's in Cornhill. There are many well-respected attendees from The Worshipful Company of Goldsmiths… well respected that is by their own community, their own circle of high-flown business but perhaps not so revered by the poor of the area. One or two onlookers, curious at the proceedings, watch from the nether reaches of the street. There are few family relatives in attendance, for the Smithsons are quite newly returned to London, having come back to the city but two years before from the Lowlands… from Holland. Hannah, who was born in London, had met Zeke in the city before the wars but they'd moved to his homeland for lack of welcome to the Dutch in England. They'd returned once the wars were over to renew his London trade as goldsmith. Hannah, in her widow's weeds, is strong, if only for her daughter Ellie who is distraught. Hann's son, Talman seems rather nonchalant, perhaps his way of containing grief, perhaps because he is older. Tally is accompanied by a friend, Kenworthy Hawker. Hawkes is a young man of gaunt appearance who had befriended Tally during an all-too-brief year at school, before the goldsmith's son had reluctantly joined his father helping with the menial daily demands of the family business. Goody Robson is at the church, ready to give solace to her friend Hannah, though the newly widowed mother seems not to need such support. As the gathered mourners leave the church, a solitary muffled bell tolls sorrowfully across Cornhill, each beat of its lament falling dead in the still air. Hann has decreed that there should be no gathering after the funeral service and coaches queue to take the gold dealers back to their precious vaults so as to allow resumption of their esteemed trade.

Goody, comforting Ellie with a much needed hug, peers across the street and there among the onlookers spies an odd character.

'Is this the very same plague-runner that Sam Bridgewater saw on that fateful night just a week or so ago?' she wonders.

Splash

And before she can look closer, a passing coach-and-four distracts her glance. When she returns to her inquisition, the figure is gone. Putting two and two together, she reaches her own conclusions.

"Dear me," she says to herself. "Surely, no good could come from that quarter. Masked like that, he has something to hide. He's surely the very one who killed poor Zeke. Someone should report him to the constables. I don't like it. I don't like it one bit."

"I've said it before… I don't like it, Master Sam," says Goody the following day.

She's visiting Sam early to see how John is. The boy has been fine this last week and is bursting with newfound enthusiasm for the river.

"*What* don't you like Goody?" asks Sam.

"That masked fellow you saw at the top of the alley the night Zeke was killed. Mark my words. That's your killer. Someone should report him to the constables."

"I don't know," says Sam. "He may be an innocent abroad. There're plenty of loons about since the plague and the fire, and not all of them with mal-intent. You should be wary of jumping to conclusions. I mean look at the rum 'un I transported across the water to Southwark that very night. He could be the one, though I wouldn't swear to it. Still, whoever it was, I'd guess it has to be someone who knew what they were after.

"So, tell me all you think may have a bearing on this unfortunate circumstance, Missus Smithson," enquires the constable who's been sent now to ask more questions for the sake of appearances and little more.

"Eliska. Please go to your room, whilst I talk with the kind gentleman. Your crewelwork will benefit from attention this morning. There's a good girl."

"Very well, mother. But I don't see why Tally doesn't have crewelwork to do."

"He's a boy, my love. And boys are not so dainty in their pastimes. He is better at fetching and carrying, though he insists on calling *that* 'cruel work'."

"Well, I sometimes wish I were a boy. I'd play at the ball and rough and tumble like *he* did at my age."

"Then you'd be full of bruises like he always was. And that wouldn't befit a lady, would it now? *You* can achieve greater, more genteel things in this life."

"I suppose so, mother."

And off the girl goes, torn between sulking and the prospect of greater things.

"Now, my man. You surely know I've told all I can to your colleague the *Parish* constable. I don't see that I can help any further."

"Perhaps not, missus, but every little detail is important if we're to catch this heinous criminal. The gallows are surely hungry for it. Now think hard again. Could anyone have borne a grudge against your Hezekiah? Or maybe this brute was simply after gold, with no premeditation of violence?"

"I've already said, and I've wracked my mind ever since, over and over, but I cannot believe anyone bore malice to my husband."

"Then desperation... or avarice perhaps... was the only

motive. Yet, you say that only two coins appear to be missing?"

"Yes. I've explained that I alone kept Hezekiah's account books and these two coins were rather special. They were gold coins of the Americas. *Aztec* Zeke called them. He'd acquired them from a dealer some months ago, a Frenchman I believe, and was hoping in due course to sell them at a good profit to some collector or other."

"So who knew, apart from you and your family, that he owned these coins?"

"I've said before that I cannot say. How can I vouch-safe that Zeke, or indeed the dealer, had not broadcast the fact to others. For my part, I had said nothing, for I know the value of prudence."

"And your children?"

"Eliska would be oblivious to them. As for Talman, he has been taught well enough not to discuss his father's business. Indeed he shows little interest in the mundanities of such things."

"And do you know where this French dealer plies his trade?"

"No. Though I recall, there was a handwritten receipt, but there was no address and it was barely legible. The name upon it was Pettifer or some such. It was some good time ago and I fear it is lost. I believe the dealer may have operated somewhere over to the west… Covent Garden way maybe."

"Very well. We shall need the receipt, if you *can* lay your hands on it. In the meantime, it may help if I ask your son a few questions, to gain *his* perspective on his father's death."

SHOOTING THE BRIDGE

"Then you shall need to return later today, for he's out arranging for the delivery of more winter coal presently. I've tried to engage him more so now, to keep his mind from grief, though he shows little appetite for errands today... indeed, poor appetite for work is not so unusual in him lately. As for the receipt, I fear that Hezekiah must have mislaid it, or else it was taken with the coins. I've searched and searched but it is nowhere to be found."

"Look here, Tally," says Kenworthy Hawker. "You can't spend your life buying coal. There's more to the world than that. Come down to Rainbow's Coffee-house over on Fleet Street with me *now*. There's good company to be had there. All the latest gossip. You'll find both high wit there and low morals. High church and low ranks. Merchants and all manner of folk. Occasionally, there's a fellow who sports the plague-mask and a much worn cloak. He seems strange, for he speaks to no one as far as I can make out and he comes and goes in a flash."

"I tried coffee and I don't much like it, Hawkes," says Tally. "It reminds me of the *koffie* in Holland. My father swore by it and drank it here in London every day... at *Garraway's* in Exchange Alley around the corner from home. The smell alone has always turned my guts and now it stinks of death for it puts me in mind of my father's demise."

"Well, friend Tally. I know your father's death remains fresh in your mind, but you really must get over it and look to your future."

"To tell the truth, Hawkes, gold turns me as much as coffee. Who would kill a man for the sake of two gold

Splash

coins?"

"You are truly naïve if you don't know the temptation, Tally. Money talks loudest of all, and gold is money. You of all people must know that."

"Maybe, but I've explained to mother. There is no way on God's earth that I could follow my father in the business of gold. It may bring wealth, but prosperity is no good if it is hollow."

"Each to his own, then. But give me wealth any day, hollow or no."

"I'd far rather visit you father's ordinary by London Wall, Hawkes. Fresh bread and salt-beef washed down with a tanker of small beer would fit the bill maybe, to drown my present melancholy."

"Then, there's The Fountain Inn just next door to Rainbow's if you prefer a tavern," persists Hawkes.

"Really, no, Hawkes. I prefer to be somewhere I know and I'm not sure what company you keep up west. I fear you may be mixing with rogues. Your sense of adventure outpaces prudence maybe."

"If we must, my friend, we'll go to father's place. But beef and ale is surely no match for coffee and conversation. And as for following fathers in their business, I could no more hawk a side of beef, salted or otherwise, than fly to the moon."

"I say you should set your sights on regarding the beauty of the moon from afar rather than thinking to fly there," says Talman. "Flying could encourage a fearful fall."

So in this mood to London Wall they go and Talman forgets all about his errand for ordering coal.

SHOOTING THE BRIDGE

"John, my boy," says Sam Bridgewater. "You're well mended now. I want you to run me an errand."

"Yes, father. Where is it and what's the errand?"

"You're to go over to Cornhill for me. To the house of Hannah Smithson. Friend Goody asked me to keep an eye out for a length of silk down at the hithes for the goldsmith's widow and I've found just the thing. She's expecting it this morning and I've wrapped it against the weather and against the sneak-thieves. Keep it close and don't dawdle lest you be waylaid."

"Don't worry, father. I'm big enough to fend for myself. Any snatchers would wish they hadn't."

"Well don't you be so cock-sure, my lad. Remember all I've told you. Just you get there and come back safe. There's no payment to collect. Goody will see to that sometime, when the widow has approved the silk."

"Very well, father."

"Here's where to find them," Sam says, showing the boy a scribbled map. Go this way look, by Walbrook. And put on your boating coat. It'll keep the package better hidden."

Off the boy dashes, full of pride at being asked on such an important errand, yet cautious enough, paying his father's words due attention. The journey proves safe, though more than once John imagines he sees pickpockets leering out of dark doorways of old, long-vacated shops or else lurking in blind alleyways. One hand is on his hidden parcel all the way, the other feeling for the reassuring handle of his secreted waterman's blade.

'Am I really big enough?' he thinks as he turns with relief into Cornhill and spies the house of Widow Smithson.

"My dear boy. Bring yourself in and sit awhile. A cooling autumn day, yet you look so hot under the collar. We'll find you beer and a little cake to refresh you whilst I peruse the silk… Eliska, where are you, my dear?" she calls out.

"Thank you, missus," says John.

"Just call me Hannah, my boy. Hannah will do. Ellie, bring cake and small beer for our young visitor, if you please. Now Ellie is rather shy, my boy, especially since we lost her father, but I'm sure you'll find her likeable."

"Yes, Missus… Missus Hannah, that is," says Johnny, blushing at this warm reception.

Ellie arrives, cup and plate in hand and, passing the beer and cake to John, curtsies shyly, yet venturing a confident stare deep into his hesitant eyes. The boy's cheeks redden all the deeper.

"Thank you," he stammers, engulfed by this vision of beautiful young innocence. Of the few young girls he has made brief acquaintances with, he has never seen such entrancing eyes, glowing like grey smoke on deep waters. And her dark-curled flowing hair, tied with a single blue ribbon. He is utterly smitten.

"Why, this material is so beautiful, my dears. Look at the clear lapis-blue and the silver traceries… filigree as fine as any your father would have set eyes upon, Ellie. It will make you a fine dress indeed, my love."

"Yes, mother. It is fine indeed," says the girl, wresting her stare from the boy.

"Your father has chosen well, my lad… John isn't it?"

"Yes Missus Hannah. Sometimes I'm called Johnny… by father and by my few friends that is."

"Then Johnny it shall be. Ellie… you must thank Johnny for your material."

"Thank you, John… Johnny. It *is* very beautiful."

The boy almost faints with elation, blushing now fit to burst.

"Now then, Johnny. Take this coin as a true thank you. You must visit again soon. Mustn't he, Ellie?"

"I suppose so, mother," the young girl offers, timidly now.

"You see, Johnny. As I said, Ellie has lost the desire for outgoing conversation this last few weeks. I'm sure a visit from you would lift her spirits and bring her out of herself."

"Yes, I expect so," says Johnny not knowing where to hide his face, his heart pounding like a hammer in his breast, "but I must go now. Father will be expecting me back."

"Perhaps on Friday next… at two of the clock, Johnny?"

"Yes, miss… I mean Hannah. If father can spare me, that is."

"We shall expect you, my boy."

He pockets the coin gratefully, bids an awkward goodbye to the two of them and bounds out into the street. His feet hardly touch the ground as he flies along the streets to home. If footpads are leering out of doorways or lurking in alleys, then John doesn't see them.

"Father! Father! I'm back," he cries, excitement brimming over. "I've delivered the silk and I've had beer and cake. And look, I've earned a coin too. The silk is for a dress for Missus Smithson's daughter, Ellie… Eliska, that is. And I've been invited to the house again."

"Have you now? Well that's well done, my boy, though I have my doubts about you drinking in new company. Have you remembered what I told you? About 'handsome is…'"

"… as handsome does, father, I know but surely this coin is handsome enough, isn't it?"

"That may well be, my boy. But if you're to go there again, I'll go with you. I'd like to check the company you're to keep. And I'd also like to be clear that you're not inviting *yourself* into their company."

"Yes, father," says Johnny, visibly subdued now, yet excited in his young being at the prospect of meeting Ellie once more.

Tally and Hawkes reach the eating-house of Jedediah Hawker by London Wall, at the sign of The Man in the Moon. The regular customers know it simply as The Moon, though some wags call it The *Loon* in the Moon, on account of Hawkes' father being the eccentric that he is. One time, Jed put up posters offering a free meal to anyone who brought in a live mermaid and he conceded the beef and cheese when a sailor brought in a wriggling squid that had been cunningly endowed with a periwig. On another occasion he offered a gratis gallon of beer to the first bringer of a talking dog and in comes a wife with her husband, he claiming that because he habitually called her a bitch, then he himself was a dog… and he certainly could talk. They downed the beer in a single sitting and walked calmly from the place, each with a steady gait. '*There*,' says the man, 'she truly *is* a bitch, for she insisted in sharing in the spoils.'

SHOOTING THE BRIDGE

"So, Talman Smithson. What's your tipple, now that you've dragged me to this den of madmen?" says Hawkes.

"I'll have beer with my food. *Small*, mind you, for I drink nothing stronger," says Tally. "But since *I've* dragged *you* here, as you so kindly put it, the charge is to be laid upon *me*. And what is your own choice, Hawkes?"

"A pint of sac, my dear. And the beef for me."

"Very well, Hawkes. I'm inclined to the hog today."

"So, you fancy a pig then, Tally? It's the best match you'll find in the place, you swine. There seems never a woman in here unless it be one with a dog of a husband and a gallon of ale or maybe a mermaid who's in truth a hirsute squid… not the prettiest of prospects, I'm sure you'd agree."

"Maybe not, but why always women with you?"

"Because the company of a lusty woman is like to the warmth of a comfortable bed… a bed with two plump pillows in which to bury your head. Now if you would come to The Fountain in Fleet Street, you'd find such a comfy bed, I assure you."

"And with it, the bed bugs no doubt."

"Not at all, my dear Tally. The women there are genteel to a fault. They do not consort with riff-raff."

"Yet they consort with *you*, Kenworthy Hawker. A rogue of the commonest sort."

"I'll have you know, my grandfather was a clergyman."

"They're the worst, I fear… womanisers all."

"So, what have you against *women*, dear Tally."

"A lot less than you, by all accounts. I suspect every inch of you is against a woman as often as is physically possible."

The two of them devour their beef and hog, washed down with copious draughts of sac and of small beer, and little more is said. But then Hawkes decides to push his point.

"How about we go to The Fountain, soon… to drink from the fount of all pleasures? You'll enjoy it. You know you will. A man of your intellect deserves to sample all things to the benefit of understanding."

Perhaps it is the drink, or perhaps it is the thirst for knowledge, the pull of intrigue, that persuades Tally to take up Hawkes' invitation to indulge.

"Very well, friend Hawkes. But only if *you* foot the bill."

"Of course, my fine fellow. What is expense to the gift of pleasure given to a good companion?"

"Talman! You really are a nuisance," screeches Hann Smithson. How could you forget the errand for coal? Sometimes I'm sure you're worth less than an empty coal cellar. Go tomorrow, without fail or else I might find the need of warming my hands on your useless backside.

"Sorry, mother. It just slipped my mind. I went to The *Loon* in the Moon with Kenny Hawker."

"That layabout? You don't need to go to The *Loon* to find a loon when Kenworthy Hawker is about. He's certainly not worthy of knowing, that one. I don't know what you see in him. It's a blessing that you only spent a year at school with him or you'd be in the Tower by now… And how *could* you forget that coal?" she chides again.

"Sorry, mother. It won't happen again."

SHOOTING THE BRIDGE

"It certainly won't. What would your father say, I wonder?"

-o-o-o-

2

Abaddon

With November on the wane, the weather is turning cold as cold. Frosts are deepening. The morning rime on the stone horse-troughs is thick and the water itself hides inaccessible under inches of ice. The streets are treacherous underfoot for man and beast alike. The usual clatter of horses and carts is accompanied by unpredicted clashes, splintering wood and tangled traces.

Today, the frost persists all day again. London is pale under a pale sky. Even beyond noon, the newly paved footways are treacherous whilst the street junctions are awash with loud argument amid a rattling chaos on the cobbles as Tally and Hawkes make their way gingerly to Fleet Street via Cheapside, Paternoster and Ludgate Hill. The sad site of the destroyed old St. Paul's is at last showing signs of revival, a happier sight now, as the new cathedral has begun to rise higher from the ashes.

"What dreadful times London has seen, Hawkes."

"It's true enough, Tally. I was just seven years old when the fire struck. Yet *we* were lucky, for The *Loon* was spared the flames. It was in the days when my father was less of a loon. I'm sure the conflagration turned his mind, you know. Either that or the fear of the plague before it."

"Of course *we* were in the Lowlands then," says Tally. "We felt the plague there when I was only four. People said the digging of new canals caused it, but in truth it surely came from the Mediterranean coast of Africa. At least *we* had no great fire caused by bakers. Indeed, we were well acquainted with disaster of a more mundane complexion, disaster caused by tulips… by a flower of all things, not by flour."

"What right-minded person would pay so much for tulip bulbs, I wonder," says Hawkes.

"Did you lose family to the plague, Hawkes?"

"No, Tally… thanks to the Devil."

"The Devil?"

"Yes. Abaddon, Satan. He is surely fallible, for he had a blind spot and didn't lay the plague upon us."

"Maybe you lay a plague upon yourself, Hawkes. This Fountain Inn sounds like the pits of Hell to me."

"No, no, my dear Tally. You have it all wrong. Soon you'll see the heavenly delights it has to offer."

They reach The Fountain, paying little regard to Rainbow's Coffee-house as they pass it. Tally is less than encouraged by a brawl between a portly, be-whiskered sailor and a skinny, hunchbacked fellow as they spill from the tavern and out into the icy road. The two of them are landing blows of a most unkind kind whilst pirouetting and tumbling unhindered in the frosty hoar with two steamy whores looking on encouraging the fray.

"You drunken bastard," complains the fat fellow, striking a blow to the nose as he curses. "You crookback

Richard, you."

"Then, if you are to give me the compliment of royalty, you should bow as low as me before calling me a bastard, you shellback," retorts the hunchback as he smacks the portly fellow in the eye.

"Landlubber!" shouts the sailor.

"Sea-blubber!" bellows the hunchback.

And so it goes on as Hawkes sidesteps the scuffle, ducks at the low doorway and enters the inn. Tally makes to follow hesitantly, eyeing the combatants with unease and the whores with consternation. As he does so, the plague-runner, emerging from Rainbow's, brushes by him, the tails of his long cloak whispering in his wake. Tally wonders if this is the very character that he'd heard Goody speaking of to his mother.

"Good day to you, sir," Tally offers as the phantom-like figure pauses. *'This odd fellow may speak little, but surely he'll respond to a friendly greeting,'* he thinks, optimistic of a reply.

Silence is the only reply, accompanied by a steely stare from two deep, dark-masked almond eyes. Then he perceives the hiss of an intake of breath and the fellow is gone. Tally shrinks back and turns, diving in through the doorway, looking to find the re-assuring company of Hawkes in the gloom.

The place reeks of sweet tobacco and sour beer. The smoke-stained ceiling is heavily bowed in places, the exposed upper floor joists beaming down at him. Tally makes out the creak of booted footfalls in some unseen corridor above, and hears occasional faint murmurings and giggles. His eyes rest on a far corner where an old salt is grinding away haphazardly at a sea shanty that no self-respecting sailor could haul a sail to. The dull clank of pewter tankards and the rattle of crude-glazed pots ring in the goldsmith's son's ears as Hawkes calls for wine.

The potent atmosphere is oppressive to Tally, for throughout the two short years the Smithsons have lived in London, he's kept himself sheltered from city life. However, he's been more adventurous of late, thanks to Hawkes, wandering further from home into unfamiliar streets. But, as strange surroundings often do, this outgoing has put him more ill-at-ease than might be warranted... after all, despite the night dangers, the day streets are not so bad a place if you know which alleys to avoid. Now, as his confidence has built, he's taken to exploring what he thinks of as the more risqué places; to the west at Smithfield Market, to the north and where lies Bedlam Hospital, and further that way to Bunhill Fields. But compared with The Fountain, seemingly the very fount of all decadence, his adventures are like a walk in the park on a fine May morning.

"Drink up, Tally, my man. This is a first-rate claret wine. Tell me what you think to it."

And, through nervousness rather than attraction, Tally downs a measure before his buds can taste it. The aftershock, to him bittersweet yet deep and rich, takes his senses by surprise. He coughs, thinking it the drink of the Devil himself, but Hawkes has refilled the mug before it reaches the counter. And so Talman is hooked, like to the first time a fish is taken from a lake merely to be put back in the water to tempt a further ensnarement by the angler. And before long, Tally has been caught so many times that the keep-net is brimming full.

"I knew you'd like it, Tally," says Hawkes, beaming proudly as an artist might present a finished portrait of his sitter.

"I'm not sure that I *do* like it, Hawkes. But it *does* seem to like *me*," replies Tally, goggle-eyed and giggle-mouthed.

Then, of a sudden, Tally's own booted footsteps are creaking along that upper corridor pursuing those murmurings, no longer faint, as he and Hawkes enter a room through a door left ajar in anticipation of their arrival. Losing his grip on this whirling world, Tally pukes violently into a convenient coal scuttle turns towards the enormous bed and, making out those two shameless whores, both of them now entangled with Hawkes and with each other, he passes out. Striking his forehead on a corner post of the bed as he falls, he hits the boards with a thud.

Friday, two of the clock, and Hannah Smithson opens her front door in answer to a bold knock.

"Why, John. You are on time. How very reliable of you," she says on seeing the young lad expectant on the top step, all spick and span like a well-groomed racehorse.

She shifts her gaze to the lower steps and there sees Sam Bridgewater, the boy's father, hovering at a distance, a hesitant chaperone.

"And this is your father then, John?"

"Yes, Hannah."

"It's Mistress Smithson, John. Be not so bold," calls Sam to his boy.

"But father...?"

"No matter, my dear Mister Bridgewater. The boy, Johnny that is, has been instructed by me in this matter. You too must call me Hannah."

"If it pleases you, dear lady. I don't wish to intrude here. Merely to see if the boy has come by your blessing and not on his own account."

"Well, I can tell you that he's more than welcome. He's a bright boy and a polite one too. And my daughter Eliska is all excitement, expecting John's visit today."

John takes to blushing once more.

"Then my job for this afternoon is done, my dear... Hannah, Though please call me Sam, if you will," says John's father, colouring the like of his boy, despite a weatherworn face."

"Sam it is. But you mustn't leave. Please come in and meet Eliska. I'm sure she will wish to thank you herself for choosing her silk... It is very beautiful."

"Of course, but then I must be back to the boat. All of London will be waiting for their transporting, and most likely looking elsewhere for it if I'm not back."

"We shall not keep you long then, Sam. But please come in for a moment or two."

And the two visitors are escorted along a poorly lit corridor into a sparsely furnished yet impressive room where is Ellie who curtsies to Sam and smiles impishly at John. The room is bright lit from a large window that looks out onto a modest garden.

"Ellie. This is John's father, Sam. He is the one who chose your silk. Perhaps a thank you is called for?"

"Thank you for the silk, sir. It is very pretty."

"It's my pleasure, young lady," says Sam. "Oh, how thoughtless of me, Hannah… I'm so sorry not to have asked. How are you managing after your tragic loss? Is there any news from the constables regarding the felon?"

"We are well enough, my dear Sam, though we've heard nothing of the criminal who stole away our Zeke. We are well supported, morally at least, by the goldsmiths of Zeke's acquaintance. And Eliska has been a courageous soul, though it has left its mark, as it has with us all. Ellie's brother, Tally, puts a brave face upon it, but I fear this plight has affected him more than a little. He is acting strangely these last few days. He's mixing with rogues I fear. He's been out all night on more than one occasion… indeed he's not returned home since yesterday morning."

And, as if summoned up by mention of his name, Talman bursts in at the street-door and bustles into the room. His forehead, cleaned now, shows evidence of his fall at The Fountain Inn."

"What in God's name, Talman?" says Hannah, full of motherly concern despite her denouncing of his ways. "What has happened? And where have you been all night?"

"Don't worry, mother," he replies furtively, nursing his head. "I stayed with Hawkes and some friends."

"And the cut on your forehead?"

"Oh, it's nothing. I caught it on a low tree branch near Rainbow's Coffee-house… over west."

"I do wish you wouldn't visit such places, Talman," complains Hannah. "And if you must, then do take care. They are places of mixed fortune."

"You know I'm always careful, mother. But there is a

world to explore. I don't intend to miss it."

"Well, care is of the essence, my lad. Just you use it."

Sam coughs discreetly.

"I'm so sorry, Sam," says Hannah, turning to the waterman. "Forgive me for ignoring you. I know you need to be away, so fare you well until we meet again. You know that you will always be welcomed here, as will young Johnny."

"Thank you, Hannah. I'll visit again when time permits."

"Well, gentlemen... and lady. That concludes the formalities of our meeting," announces James Otway, goldsmith. "It is a great privilege that you have accorded, for me to preside over this gathering here in our restored hall. Surely the Great Fire has been as big a challenge to us as that of the Stuart monarch's placing such a heavy call upon our very existence... and yet we thrive."

"Hear him! Hear him!" implores Kaleb Tasker, fellow goldsmith. "And we must continue to thrive by all means possible. Surely, after all, the nation banks upon us."

Kaleb Tasker is a dour fellow, and appears disgruntled even when at his happiest. If he makes a profit, then in his own mind he is bound to lose it and if he makes a loss, then that loss can only multiply in his thoughts.

"True words indeed, Tasker. We must indeed thrive," agrees Otway. "Though, whilst of tradition we may be men of means, I trust we are not *mean* men. And mindful of this, I wish to say a few words of condolence to our honorary guest, the Widow Smithson."

Hannah Smithson, nods in silent acknowledgement.

Whilst she is determined to continue her late husband's trade, she is not an accepted member of The Guild, and is unlikely to be accorded that concession.

"You will all agree, that Hezekiah's demise has visited a great loss on us all, and I propose that for the time being, Hannah here be accorded honorary admission to our guild... perhaps until her son, Talman can complete an apprenticeship. We would of course wish to support him in this."

"Well, I wonder if we can afford such niceties, in these difficult times?" asks Tasker. "The king may wish us drained but we need no assistance in such a direction from a woman."

"You need not trouble yourself, sir," Hannah responds, taking the fractious Tasker to task. It is *I* that will continue with my poor husband's business, with or without the support of this guild. In any case, I fear my son would no sooner take to an apprenticeship with The Guild than he would wish to become a gong-farmer, sir."

"A what?" stutters Tasker, taken aback by this unseemly barb... from a *woman* of all things.

"Now, now, gentlemen... err gentleman and lady," interjects James Otway. "Are we to stoop to the rhetoric of the House of Commons? I trust not."

"A gong-farmer, sir! A turd-shoveller. Is your nose so elevated as to prevent your knowing what happens to your night soil?" says Hannah, persisting in her annoyance with Tasker. "Like us all, *you* produce shit sir... but from both ends it seems."

And with this, she storms out of the meeting, to the accompaniment of supportive cheers from all the assembled company... all that is except for Tasker, who is red-faced fit to burst and not entirely clear as to why the widow is so affronted. Otway displays an ambivalent expression, a combination of amusement and embarrassment.

"Talman, my dear. I confess that I suffered a deal of discomfiture yesterday on your behalf. I told the meeting of The Guild that you wouldn't be interested in a place in their company."

"But mother, why would you do such a thing? I'm sure I'd make an excellent goldsmith."

"You'd make an excellent goldsmith weep, more like. Time and again you've hinted your distaste for the trade, and with your ever more wayward attitude, you'd do more damage even than King Charles. The Goldsmiths' Company is troubling to me, despite their professed support, but the company *you* are keeping of late is like to lead to disaster, my boy."

"You mean Hawkes, mother? Why, he's an influence for good, *I* say. He's a worldly man and a wily fellow, bent on success."

"No, Tally. He's a wild man, willy-nilly and bent on excess."

"That's unfair, mother, and you know it is. Why, he is opening my eyes to a world of love and expression. I am to go to the theatre with him this very day."

"Well there's the nub, Talman. The theatre can teach you many things, but be warned, its illusory glamour presents a fork in the road... a subtle choice between your coming upon good lore or else upon bad encounters with

Abaddon

the law. Be sure you choose wisely, my boy… for *my* sake *and* for your sister's. And spend your allowance with prudence, for we all need prudence now."

"I understand, mother, though I fear your apprehensions are built on myth."

"That's as maybe, but I've seen actors and audience alike carried away on theatre's flippant nonsense… carried from the bright-candled footlights only to be snuffed out in some dreadful, dark place or other."

"I'm sure you worry needlessly, mother dear."

And with this, Tally takes up his hat and a silver-topped cane and out he goes into the street to meet up with his mentor, Hawkes.

Cornhill is still in the grip of deep frost and the cane proves a fine aid to verticality for Tally. A vaguely vagrant old fellow, wrapped in clothing at once warm and worn, sits at the foot of neighbouring entrance steps. It seems he has slipped from the higher graces of life and is nursing bruised knees, recovering from a more present fall from grace after near collision with a passing horse and carriage. The carriage is disappearing along the nether reaches of Cheapside as Tally negotiates the wincing obstruction in his path.

"Are you quite alright, my man?" he offers the vagabond of a fellow, rather more charitably than might be expected of the errant youth.

"Yes, your lordship," bleats the bruised individual. "At least there's nothing wrong but for what a coin for hot grog wouldn't cure. A cripple needs hot grog now and then, sir."

SHOOTING THE BRIDGE

"But you've been a cripple for but a few moments… a temporary cripple at that."

"Well yes, sir… but then hot grog is only temporary too ain't it, good sir. And life itself is only temporary you know… *tempus futile* is what the Latinos call it."

"Perhaps you mean *Tempus Fugit*?"

"That too."

Tally chuckles at the humorous bundle of baggage, throws him a penny, then steps out gingerly on his frosty way in the direction of Fleet Street in the wake of the offending coach, not thinking for a moment upon the sage words of the odd fellow.

"Thank you, sir," calls the old man. "'Be kind to the world and it'll return the favour', is what I always say," and clutching afresh at his shins, he mumbles: "Ouch, by God! I just wish the world and that damned coach were in accord with each other."

In truth he'd been wishing for years that he'd followed the maxim… before the very world had turned against him.

Tally is meeting Hawkes at The Fountain Inn with a view to the pair of them travelling on to Dorset Gardens where is The Duke's Theatre. As he makes his approach to the inn he rubs his forehead with some trepidation, his unfortunate encounter with the bedpost brought to mind. No brawling sailor, no fighting hunchback, no steaming whores. No grinding sea shanty this time around… *'Maybe they're all in congress… or else I imagined the whole mad company?'* he smiles to himself… *'Now there's a thought, indeed. Who needs the illusion of theatre when there's a place the like of The Fountain?'*

Tally is nervous, despite the apparently benign environment of the inn today. Hawkes is yet to make his appearance and the shifty landlord eyes the goldsmith's son suspiciously, rattling tankards as if hinting at Tally's failure to buy a drink.

"I'm waiting for a friend, landlord. Kenworthy Hawker... Hawkes. I'm sure you know him, don't you?"

"Know him? Why the entirety of Fleet Street knows Hawkes. Indeed they know him from Bagnigge to the Thames and from Drury Lane to St. Paul's, for their sins."

"Well, he's overdue and he should be here at any moment."

"Don't be too sure. Hawkes is a law unto himself, that one. Wait a minute... I remember you now... you were here with him not so long ago... you damaged my bedpost, you did. I'm minded to charge you for the repairs."

"Not half as much as it damaged me. Look at this here cut."

"Blimey! No wonder the bedpost was splintered. Still, I'm only joking about the repairs. I think it survived. It's seen a lot more action than that in its time. My girls can get quite carried away you know."

"Really?"

"I've known clients with splinters big as a... well I won't say what."

"Tally! Well met, my friend," calls out Hawkes as he sweeps in over the threshold. "Sorry I'm late. My father the loon waylaid me. He was complaining that a firkin from the brewer came empty... but in truth he'd sent the full one back himself by mistake."

"Truly tragic, Hawkes. How you must rue his behaviour."

"Well, it *is* true. His progressing lunacy is a tragedy indeed. I suppose it comes to us all in one form or another, so sympathy is fitting."

"Actually, I meant all that ale gone away without it put to good use."

"You heartless sot, Tally. You're obviously keeping bad company."

"Well *you* know the company I keep better than I, Hawkes. You eat and sleep with him after all. A mirror reveals him to you every morning, does it not?"

"Then I have to say you keep *good* company, my dear Tally. And speaking of company, the Duke's Company awaits us. We go to see Abdelazer, The Moor's Revenge. It's a tragedy by Astrea who in truth is Aphra Benn... a woman."

"A woman, Hawkes? How the world changes, thanks to King Charlie. A wise trend no doubt, for we all know from life itself what accomplished actors women can be."

"They say she's the king's spy, or was... against the Dutch," says Hawkes.

"Be careful, Hawkes. Life in the Lowlands was dear to me... perhaps dearer than the lowlife here in London."

"Well, I'm sure we can call a truce now that the wars are over, can we not? Though it occurred to me... could your father's killer have been someone with a grudge against you Cloglanders."

"I don't believe that for a minute, Hawkes. They were simply after gold... and particular items of gold at that... the *Aztec* coins my father had acquired."

"Anyway, you'll love the theatre, Tally," says Hawkes, bringing the subject back to the matter in hand. "Through the magic of the players and the scenic wonders you'll be brought to life like Lazarus himself."

"Steady, Hawkes. Anyone would think I'm dead to the world. I can take the world on equal terms quite as well as you. And as for players… how can *they* represent true life?"

"So, you doubt their skill, do you? Well prepare for a surprise. Suspend disbelief and be carried on a wave of adventure to the tragic heat of Spain and Africa."

"Could you not find us a comedy? Life is tragic enough without giving it fanfare."

"Maybe next time, Tally. But for now let's be tragically entranced."

The two young men make now for Dorset Gardens, taking shortcuts through oppressive, winding alleys. Passing close by the old Templars' Church and on to Whitefriars, a tangible anticipation builds step by step ahead of them and a hubbub grows by degrees in their ears. They make out the street-criers touting their wares. There are pie-men with steaming trays fresh from the ovens, oyster sellers and fortune-tellers. Then there are card tricksters and cutpurses, acrobats, clowns with false noses and quacks with false medicines, street musicians and ham actors rehearsing for fame. Then come the hussies, some whores, some merely brazen flirts. And all of them keen to offload their tempting goods and entertainments on the wealthy or the foolish. Carriages and coaches are queuing,

SHOOTING THE BRIDGE

occasional Sedan chairs weaving, and all is wrapped up in a chaos of ribbons and pennants.

Inside the theatre, the stale scents of ale and oranges and sweat build mingling. Talman is agog at the spectacle before him on the candlelit stage, and the story begins:

The Moor, intent on revenge for the killing of his father when he was but a boy, puts Tally in mind of his own father, taken from him but recently by some cruel assailant who has slipped away into the anonymity of London, all for the want of gold.

When the Moor seduces the Spanish queen, avenges his father with the killing of the king and beguiles the royal princess into the bargain, Tally imagines wreaking such a trail of destruction himself; he would find and slay the mysterious French dealer who supplied the coins and who in so doing sowed the seeds of theft, he would ensnare all the rogue's family into subservience and he would take all the dealer's possessions too.

At the last, the Moor's fantastical spree is over and his over-zestful pride leaves him to die a hollow death. Tally is content now, knowing in his heart that he would never dare attempt avenging anyone or anything... knowing that his true response to the slaying of his *own* father is merely turning him, through Hawkes, towards the alehouses and whorehouses of a drab and depressing London... the London that awaits him outside the confines of this theatrical, fantastical plot.

As Tally and Hawkes make to leave, the goldsmith's son feels the swish of a cloak as a shadowy figure brushes by them, making for the nearest exit.

"Hawkes… it's that damnable plague-runner. He haunts us everywhere we go, it seems. Quick, let's see where he's bound."

And before Tally knows it, Hawkes is out in the street, fighting to free his right arm which is in his friend's firm grip. The pair of them hurry down side streets and alleys in pursuit of the mysterious masquerader.

"You must have seen this fellow many times before now, Hawkes. He seems to be everywhere," pants Tally, breathlessly.

"I've seen him, it's true. But he never speaks… always points his order for food and drink… always disappears without a by-your-leave," Hawkes informs Tally, gasping now for air.

Skirting the burying ground at Bridewell and scurrying into another drab alley, the two of them lose sight of their quarry for a moment. As they re-emerge into daylight they find themselves confronted by the Fleet Ditch. At the open corner of the alley sits a nondescript coffee-house, not a customer in sight except for the mysterious cloaked and masked fellow who is sat calmly at a far table in a corner as if he's been there all day. They enter, cautious. There's no sign of a proprietor and the counter is dusty and dim-lit with one candle. A black cat, rare since the killing sprees during and since the plague, slinks by them and out into the street. Tally is determined to confront the shadowy and elusive masked fellow once and for all. He sits himself down at the occupied table, facing the mask, and stares into those deep almond eyes. The eyes stare back silent, unblinking, the whites enhanced by swarthy lids untouched by age and all but hidden in the depths of the mask's eyeholes.

"Who *are* you?" demands Tally.

Silence.

Hawkes now drags a chair, its feet screeching on the bare boards, and places it beside his friend. He sits down as silent as the mask.

"Who *are* you?" insists Tally.

Silence still.

He makes a lunge for the mask, tearing it off in one swift move, displacing the hood of the cloak as he does so. Dark flowing hair falls around a fair face and down upon the shoulders of the cloak. Tally sits back bolt upright in his chair as the woman bares her teeth with a hiss. And in the same breath, a curved dagger is thrust into the eye-line of the surprised Tally, stretched at arm's length to within an inch of his nose. The blade glints in a single beam of sunlight that's streaming in through a high window, escaping from the day into the dusky shop… if shop it can be called. Hawkes sits impassive as if expecting this fierce reaction.

"You… You're a woman!" exclaims Tally, with a shrill.

"Perceptive," she replies. "But I don't take kindly to people who snatch, perceptive or not."

"I'm sorry, truly sorry," says Tally, smitten by the capricious vision of dark beauty before him. "I would buy you refreshment but there seems to be no one to serve. Either way, we must talk."

Her cover undone, she picks up her mask, places it on the table and loosens her tongue, cautiously withdrawing the glinting blade from the tip of Tally's nose.

"He'll be about somewhere. Probably out in the yard

feeding the rats with yesterday's leftovers. The cat does its best to catch the vermin but *he* feeds them up fit to burst. I sometimes wonder if he serves them up on trenchers."

Hawkes sits on the edge of the conversation, seemingly reluctant to join it.

"Look," says Tally to the dark beauty, "I'm Talman. They call me Tally, and this here is Hawkes. What name are you known by?"

Hawkes fidgets apprehensively.

"Well then, Tally my fine friend. I *know* Kenworthy Hawker. At least I know him well enough. Everyone does… though I doubt he knows me."

Hawkes fidgets ever more uneasily at this rehearsal of his name.

"As for *my* name, I prefer to keep the truth of it to myself. You may call me Jebila, if you must have a name. It is where I'm from… in Tangier."

"I see. So is this why you were at the play? The Moor… of course," says Tally, in a burst of realization.

"As I said, you are indeed perceptive. Though my interest in the play is a passing one."

"Then why are you in London?"

"I came here but six months ago, against my will, on a trading ship from France. It is a long story and you need not know the details. It is enough to say that the French pig who brought me here is a slaver. The poor souls he ships are treated ill and now no doubt they're either dead or enslaved to the gentry, maybe here in your precious England or in The West Indies. For my part, I am no slave, but was caught up in their cause and might as well have been. If I had not used my guile and escaped the French slaver's clutches when we arrived here, I would likely have been enslaved to *him*. I could *kill* the pig."

"The Moor's Revenge," ventured Hawkes at last.

"No. In truth I seek no revenge. But for now I'm forced by circumstance to stay here in London, though once I'm able I'm minded to return to my dear Africa."

"But surely, the mask and cloak can only bring attention to you."

"They do, but people stay at a distance, fearing the connotation of plague. And, as you have found, those who come too close are apt to feel the breath of my blade. I stay away from the docks, for that is where the slave trader is likely to be found and in truth I have no wish to confront him. And the customs men at the docks may have some ill fate in mind for me too, if they can but catch my identity."

"Then, if you wish to remain unknown, why tell *us* all this now?" asks Tally.

"You leave me little choice with your wild snatching. Thanks to you I'll now be known as woman, not as man."

"But, for my part, you can rely on your secret being kept," Tally assures the African beauty. What about you, Hawkes? You can keep this cloak-and-dagger clandestine, can't you?"

"If it must be so," says Hawkes, mindful of the blade.

Truth be known, Tally is thinking that there may be links here to his father's death, though he is reluctant to take a route into the shady world of slavers and blades. *'Am I still in a fantastical play here?'* he thinks.

"I'll never trust Hawker here any further than I can throw my cloak around my shoulders… I've seen what he is capable of. And as for you, Talman, I'm not sure that I can trust *you* either. If we are to meet again on friendly terms, then keep my secret… the both of you. I may prove more useful to you, Talman Smithson, than you might ever guess."

And with this, her silk-black hair is stowed afresh inside her hood, the mask is placed over that fair countenance once again and in the swish of a cloak she is out the door and gone."

"But, I didn't tell her that Smithson is my name?" says Tally to his companion.

"Er… what?" says Hawkes, barely snapping out of the trance he is in.

"Never mind, dear Hawkes. Never you mind."

At last, Hawkes breaks his trance, woken from his woolgathering by the squeal of a kicked cat.

"Can I help you with your needs, gentlemen?" asks the diminutive, greasy fellow that has appeared out of the murky depths of the building as if from the lamp of Ala al-Din.

He wipes his greasy hands on his greasy apron.

"No. No, thank you kindly, my friend," says Hawkes. "We were just looking for a friend, but we appear to have missed him."

The two of them make haste to the door, Tally stumbling into Hawkes' chair and almost spread-eagling onto the bare boards, Hawkes tripping over the threshold, and out into blue daylight they tumble.

-o-o-o-

3

A Fair Frost for a Frost Fair

The frosty weather persists for days and weeks, frost on frost, ice on ice. The horse-troughs are soon thick as thick with ice and every morning the ostlers and the stable lads persuade water to the surface with hammers and picks. Full into winter now, snow sets in and freezes solid on the roads and footways. Slush attempts to get a grip, but freezes too, even when salt is spread. Horses, carts and carriages all find their journeys perilous and traffic grinds along precarious slow, all but defeated.

Then one day Sam sees what he'd feared most of all. On the west side of the bridge, where the water is sluggish, ice is forming inch by inch. Then, over several days, it creeps back westwards, past Steelyard, past Queenhythe and on by Paul's Wharf to Blackfriars Stairs.

"Dear Jesus," he says to John. "If this weather continues, we shall starve to death, if not from hunger then from cold."

"But, we *do* have coal father."

"We do, John. And we shall *need* it too. But a mountain of burning coal wouldn't thaw the river. And with ice all about us we shall have no fares, I fear. People will take to walking from here to Southwark… the bridge won't be the only way across. Believe you me, I know."

"But father, we could make *your* boat into a sled and glide to and fro on the ice."

"Others have tried. But even though we've added mast and sail to the boat this past while, you must remember that the wind is not an easy servant."

"Then we could use the oars, or poles, to push us."

"We shall see, lad. And if ever the day comes when I am desperate, we can always try. Even so, when needs must we mustn't give in to need without a thought. I've told you before, haven't I, that this has happened more than once in the past. The last time was some good few years ago now, around the time of the Fire… when you were just four years old and we'd lost your mother. Her death was an icy blast to me, and I still feel the chill of it now."

"You *have* told me of the frozen river, father."

"That's as maybe, but it's worth a reminder, John. You won't have felt the icy blast of the weather yourself, for I kept you warm at home. But out in the wide city, on the river, the people took to skating… for need *and* for pleasure. Then tradesmen set up stalls in a ribbon along the frozen waters. And in this way, a Fair grew. It was a city full of sore backsides, *I* can tell you. And worse… broken bones and the occasional disappearance of fat men through thin ice. For a week or two the freeze was tolerable and in some ways entertaining, but it became a serious matter, for it went on too long. Last time, mad folk even brought horses onto the ice, and they lit bonfires on raised platforms too. It became a carnival of sorts. Then a

SHOOTING THE BRIDGE

thaw set in and the carnival became macabre... ice cracking unexpectedly and people lucky if they escaped drowning. And there was a mad rush to remove the entire hotchpotch; the sailcloth stalls and their poles and pennants, the trestles, the lanthorns, the pigs and the poultry. And the bonfires were left to sink by quickening degrees into the thawing depths."

And now once again, for weeks on end, the ice takes a grip on London. People will not venture out on a whim in the dreadful cold and no river carrying is to be had. Sam and his boy fare well enough at first, and without the need for a sailing sled, turning their hands to other tasks; mending roofs, chopping wood, carrying coal. But things are getting tight.

"I'll be looking for temporary work in the boatyards. I have a friend in a sea captain I know. He works out of Botolph Wharf, down near the Custom House. He has a couple of heavy barges and they're always in need of some repair or other. I've worked for him before on them, when need has left us wanting."

Meanwhile, John, with his father close by, had sampled the madness of a Frost Fair and all the mayhem, at times merry and at times miserable, that the deep freeze brings with it; booted and scarved revellers, despondent watermen, gentry and paupers alike laughing and crying in their turns.

"John, my boy," calls Sam to his son. "Hold fast to our work for a while. I have an errand to run."

"Yes, father. How long will you be gone?"

A Fair Frost for a Frost Fair

"I hope an hour at most if the bridge will allow it, though I fear it could be a while longer. With the water crossings frozen and all the chaos of traffic in the streets, who knows? What we need in truth is a further bridge, but the country can't afford it. England's coffers are depleted by the wars and now we're paying for it in congestion. The bridge we have is like the neck of a bottle… the wine won't flow as easy as it should, unless it should be a gentle flow. But we continue to fill and empty the bottle at the same time… and a bottle needs a way out for the wine and a way by for the air replacing it."

Sam has been working these last few days down at Botolph Wharf and when not employed there, he and Johnny are making good use of their dwindled trade in repairing their own boat, ready for a renewed onslaught once the ice has gone. Sam's craft is recently fitted with mast and sail that are now safely stowed in their modest shed. The boat itself is hauled up outside, tipped keel over rowlocks for fresh proofing against the water. The smell of boiling tar is everywhere as many of the watermen take like advantage of the lull in business. John is enjoying the messy job of applying the tar to the upturned hull, his brush soon clogged to uselessness by the congealing black stuff.

"Then bring fresh brushes, father. This one is good for little now."

"Use mine for the moment, John. I'll make sure we have new ones."

Sam is off to visit a bookshop on the bridge. He has in mind a book he's seen there some days before. The waterman reads but little, for his sparse education will not

SHOOTING THE BRIDGE

allow it. He'd barely learned his letters and, in truth, has little need for reading or for writing. The book is illustrated prettily and is intended as a present… a present for Hannah Smithson. He's struck up something of a friendship with her and intends to visit the following day.

By the time Sam reaches the bridge it's approaching midday. He was not wrong in anticipating the turmoil. Much of the ice has been cleared from the decking, but the sheer amount of traffic, both wheeled and pedestrian would be enough to frustrate speedy passage even if it were well policed… and policed it is not. Carriage drivers are all vying for spaces that are far too narrow to accommodate their vehicles. Horses are panicking and shying. Pedestrians are haphazard and inconsiderate in their progress, all for the want of saving a minute or two here or there. The houses and the shops and other public places built upon the bridge are a marvel indeed but, in narrowing the way, they only serve to make the present madness yet more insane.

'*Thank the Lord for the river. On normal days at any rate,*' thinks Sam. '*The street on the bridge is best avoided at all but the quietest of times, I tell my customers. And today, I can see it would be good advice.*'

Sam weaves his way around stuck carts and faltering horses, Sedan chairs, fellow foot-fallers and all. One poor fellow and his helpers are driving a flock of sheep of all things. The sheep are bound for market north of the river and their bedlam of noise rises as they approach Sam and falls as they pass him, finally beating their bleating way to the city end of the bridge.

'*Maybe we shouldn't have protested at the proposal to build a*

A Fair Frost for a Frost Fair

second bridge up at Westminster after all,' he thinks.

Once he reaches his destination, Sam slips into the refuge of the bookshop, forcing open the door against the press of the crowd. The door slams shut behind him.

"Thank God for that," he says, reaching for a kerchief and wiping his sweating brow.

The bookseller greets Sam with a sour smile, looking at his pocket watch as he does so. The hands are just past the meridian.

"Good afternoon, sir."

"Quiet today isn't it?" says Sam sardonically.

"If only you knew, sir. Trade is slower than you might imagine. I don't know what the world is coming to. There was a time when the book trade thrived, but somehow people, even the gentry, seem more content to drink their time away in the alehouses or coffee-houses than they do to sit at home and leaf through the pages of a book. Just look out there… where on earth are they all bound? As far as I can fathom, it is a pointless congestion, charging here and charging there for the flimsiest of reasons."

"Well, I suppose they all have their business to attend to, my dear man," suggest Sam, sympathetic both to the bookseller and to the traffic.

"I imagine you're right, my friend. Now what can I do for you?"

"I am keen to purchase the book of poems which you have in your window. And since your trade is not brisk, I expect a good price."

"There, you see. The few people, like you, who are prepared to read more than a broadside ballad want it at a knockdown price."

SHOOTING THE BRIDGE

"Oh it's not for me. It's for a lady friend. And I can ill afford too much myself for, as a waterman, *my* trade is slack too at present, thanks to the ice."

"Then I suppose we must do what we can," says the bookseller, reaching for the volume from his window. "I'll stand ten percent but no more. And if I see you on the river henceforth, I'll expect the same."

"Then you have a deal, my man."

They shake hands and money is exchanged. The purchase is carefully wrapped and Sam bids the shopkeeper good day as another customer forces his way into the shop, re-adjusting his peruke which has been dislodged by the heaving masses outside.

"Good afternoon, Mister Pepys," offers the bookseller. "What is it today?"

"I believe you have a particular broadsheet ballad that I'm minded to acquire… at the right price mind you."

Sam smiles to himself as he leaves the shop clutching his purchase, ready to do battle back to the city side and to find new brushes for Johnny and himself.

A loud knock at the door brings Hann Smithson from her conversation with Goodwife Robson so as to answer.

"Oh, Mister Otway. What a pleasant surprise to see you. Please do come in," says Hannah, disguising her anguish that a member of The Guild should visit so informally.

She escorts him into the room where is Goody.

"Oh, I see you already have company, Mistress Smithson. Perhaps I should call another time. I feel my errand is somewhat delicate."

"Please don't fret, James. Goody here is my very best of

A Fair Frost for a Frost Fair

friends and I'm sure she is the soul of discretion in all things."

Hannah says this, not believing it herself for one moment, but ready to share this encounter with her good friend regardless of delicacy.

"Well then, my dear Mistress Smithson," says the goldsmith. "Forgive my calling unannounced, but I felt it only fair to come and apologize for the recent behaviour of our Mister Tasker. He is apt to regard himself with an elevated importance well above his true position in The Guild. We *do* have our problems with him, and I would hate you to think that he is the foundation of our policies."

"Well, perhaps my outburst was beyond appropriate itself."

"No, no good lady. He needed to be put in his place and has been a little more conciliatory since his encounter with you. I feel you have served us a favour… for the time being at least. I think I speak for all of us goldsmiths, apart from the one antagonist, when I say that we are keen as ever to support you through your difficulties."

"You are most kind, James. And should I find myself in difficulties, I will of course avail myself of your assistance. But I can assure you that Hezekiah's insightful investments have left me well able to survive my present trepidations."

At this point, Hannah is spared her embarrassments at the visit, by the agitated arrival of her son, Talman.

"Very well, my dear. I can see that you have a busy day of it. I shall leave you to it."

"I thank you for your consideration, James. I shall contemplate attending the next meeting of The Company, though I do not relish the prospect of crossing words with friend Tasker again. Goody will show you out."

"Now then, Tally," says Hann, "what is it *this* time? I can see that you are disquieted over something or other."

"Well, mother. I haven't mentioned it before now, for I've been turning the thing over in my mind," he says hesitantly. "But when Hawkes and I went to the theatre a while ago, a strange thing happened…"

He hesitates.

With the goldsmith gone, Goody returns to the room.

"Well?" says Hannah, encouraging Tally to continue.

Goody listens in, discreet at the other side of the room yet intent on picking up some gossip or other. And Tally, despite the pleas of Jebila that he and Hawkes keep her secrets concealed, spills the story of the confrontation with the plague-runner. Goody stifles a cough at the mention of the masker and her ears are all the sharper when Tally tells of Tangier and the slave trader.

"And I've been agonizing… could this French slaver be the very dealer that sold father those coins, I wonder?"

"I doubt it, Tally. I believe the dealer trades near Covent Garden somewhere. I can't imagine that a slaver would put down such roots. Surely, he'd be furtively bound to his boat and the docks. You'd better forget the encounter, dear Tally. Your imagination is running ahead of you. Tear yourself away from Hawkes and these wild encounters or you will regret it. What's done is done and we need to look to the future."

The following day, Goody Robson finds herself in the back-alley on Garlick Hill where is home for Sam and

Johnny. She's fit to burst with yesterday's gossip and can't wait to tell our Sam.

"Well, Master Sam. I must say, Hannah is doing her best in the circumstance of her widowhood but yesterday she had a visit from one of her goldsmith fellows. Otway… James Otway was his name. Apparently she had a good old confrontation with one of them at a meeting… Tasker, *his* name is. But that's not the interesting thing."

"Johnny, go to the shed for coal will you?"

"Yes father," his son replies, obedient but reluctant to miss Goody's revelations.

"You know the masker that's been spotted about," Goody continues. "Well, young Tally saw him… or I should say *her*. The masker is a *woman* of all things. Jebila she calls herself and she comes from some foreign place. Tangier, I think she said. And she came here on a slave ship."

"This all sounds very fantastical, Goody. Are you sure you've not been emptying the barrel?"

"No, I have *not*, Master Sam. How could you *say* such a thing?"

"I jest, Goody. But if your tale be true then you'd better not mention this around and about or you may bring unnecessary trouble to your door. I'm intending to visit Hannah myself later today and I shall have a quiet word with her. She can do without all this aggravation from her son… or from anyone else for that matter."

"Oh, you're visiting Hannah. And why would that be, I wonder?"

"Never you mind, Goody. Never you mind. You be home now, and keep you hushed."

SHOOTING THE BRIDGE

"Now then, Johnny. Goody's gone on her way and I need you to run us an errand. The spare boat-sail needs repair, so we can be full ready for the river come the thaw. There's a small tear that'll soon be a large tear if we don't see to it. We need patching material from Harrison on Ebbgate Lane, close by Swan Stairs. Tell him it's for me… he'll do us a good price on a yard of flaxen… flax mind you, not hemp. And don't get Dutch material… I'll not have *Duck* on the boat. *Duck* from the Lowlands did more than enough damage in the wars. Bloody Dutch."

"But aren't Hannah and Ellie Dutch, father?"

"That's different, lad."

"In what way, father?"

"Well, Dutch *sails* are strong but far too coarse, while Dutch *women* are strong and rather more refined… well, Hannah is anyway, don't you think?"

"I suppose so, but then the women don't have to weather storms do they?"

"Don't you believe it, my boy. Hannah is weathering her own storm at the moment, and weathering it well as far as I can tell. Just like *we've* had to weather the storm without your mother."

"Is Ellie weathering a storm too?"

"I suppose she is, John. She must miss her father a great deal. And that brother of hers is no substitute for a father from what I can make out. Anyway, you ask too many questions."

"Then I won't ask why *you're* not going to Harrison's."

"Well, if you must know, I'm off to see Hannah. I have something for her."

"What is it? Can I come? To see Ellie?"

A Fair Frost for a Frost Fair

"I *did* say you ask too many questions, and you do. Maybe you can come next time if you must. And anyway you can go there on your own betimes, if you don't make a nuisance of yourself, can't you?"

"Very well. Then tell them I shall go to see them tomorrow, if you can spare me father."

"I shall *ask* for you, not *tell* them. And if they are willing, you can go after noon, when we've mended that sail."

"Shall I take the money for payment then, father?" asks Johnny risking another, though rather more essential question happy now in anticipation of a visit to Ellie.

"No, Tell Harrison credit. He won't mind."

"Perhaps I should *ask* him, father. Not *tell* him."

"I'm glad you're taking note, John."

And away the boy goes.

"Why, Samuel Bridgewater, it is so beautiful. The engravings are the most magical that I've set eyes upon and I'm sure the poems will be as enchanting. Where did you find it?"

"Oh, I'm sure they will be, Mistress Hannah," says Sam, a little embarrassed at her response to his gift and not knowing for sure if the poems were suited or otherwise as a present for a lady of some standing. "I found it in the bookshop on the bridge."

"This must have cost you a pretty penny, my dear Sam. Tell me, what have I done to deserve such consideration?"

"It's simply that I perceive your anguish, despite the brave face you put upon your grief. It's really just to bring you some cheer."

SHOOTING THE BRIDGE

"Then it's not intended to admit you to my favour, Sam?" Hann Smithson says this with a hint of mischief, though also mindful of Sam's surprisingly direct approach.

"Of course not Hannah. I merely wish it as a token of friendship."

"Indeed, it is a token that is appreciated and it will be treasured, I assure you. As for my grief… I thought it well hidden, but you have a keen eye, my dear man."

"It comes from being on the river, Hannah. A waterman without a keen eye brings no good to his customers *or* himself… a keen eye for the unnatural and a weather eye for the natural."

"Well, it's true that I grieve for the loss of my Zeke and I feel I always shall. But it's more for the want of confidence that Talman might weather our new circumstance. He seems ever more to be in the grip of that awful Kenworthy Hawker and I fear no good will come of their escapades."

"Surely young Talman will find a sensible path. I imagine it's all part of his learning the ways of this world."

"But Sam. Only yesterday he related a worrying tale to me. It appears that he went to the theatre some time ago and fell upon an odd encounter. He came across the plague-runner there and confronted her… for it is a woman, Sam… some exotic creature from Morocco he tells me."

"Hannah. I have to confess… I've already learned of this."

"Ah, our good friend Goody, no doubt. My, how quickly she moves with her gossip. But she is well meaning and I can only blame myself for her being a party to this affair."

"Well, I've cautioned her to be quiet about it, unless she wants to get caught up in dark affairs," says Sam.

"And I shall do the same, Sam. When next I see her."

"I have to say, Hannah, that from what Goody told me, this enigmatic masked woman seems less the hunter and more the preyed upon. Yet there's more than a hint in her story of what Tally is thinking… of unscrupulous dealers and murderous robbery. Perhaps I should speak with Talman on your behalf to see if there's anything I can do to explore this bizarre story further. It may unearth your husband's killer."

"But, it could be a dangerous world you are peering into, Sam. I wouldn't want to send you on such a path. What's done is done and nothing will bring Zeke back to us."

"Yet justice should be attempted, Hannah. And the constables seem to have exhausted their feeble attempt at it."

"Then, should *they* be told of all this?"

"I doubt they'd be at all interested, Hannah. The crimes thrown up in this dreadful city at every hour of every day overwhelm them and in these latter days they so often close the books as soon as close a door. At least let me explore a little and then we shall see."

"But where will you search, Sam? London is a big place… and oft a terrifying one when provoked."

"It's true, Hann, and its underworld is like to the hidden depths of an iceberg and just as perilous, but I think you are owed justice, my dear."

"Sam, dear friend, I would rather justice were left to lament its own demands than for you to come to harm on my behalf."

"Well, Hannah, if justice were left to that, then the world would lose what little control it has. First of all I must speak with Tally and his friend Hawkes. I need to know more of their encounter with this Jebila from Tangier. And there may be ties with the docks in all this. I *know* the wharfs and I'm more comfortable than many in the inns and taverns there. I've been employed down at Botolph Wharf lately and it wouldn't be out of place for me to make an innocent enquiry or two. And it's surprising what you learn if you just keep your eyes wide and your ears even wider."

"Don't you go trusting that Hawkes, Sam. I'm sure he's the very Devil, and you won't find him *here*... I forbade Talman from bringing him into our home."

"I'm used to bigger villains than Hawkes, my dear Hann. He's just a wayward young fellow from what I can tell."

"Well, if he's taken a wayward path in life, he's surely dragging Talman down the wrong fork in the road with him."

"Don't you fret, Hannah. All will come good in the end," Sam assures her. "Do you know where Tally is now?"

"Over at The Man in the Moon I shouldn't wonder, Sam. It's Hawkes' father's place. I think my son has always preferred it to the more iniquitous places his wayward companion chooses to frequent."

"Oh, The *Loon* is it? That place is peculiar enough,

though more innocent than the likes of The Bear or The Magpie at the foot of the bridge. At least it's at a distance from the rough trades."

"I wish you luck with Talman. I can't seem to fathom his mind these days."

"Well, Hannah, don't mention my quest to Tally, but let me know when he next hints that he's off there and maybe I'll catch them both then."

And so it is, later that same week, that Sam turns up at The *Loon*.

"What shall you have, my friend," asks Jed Hawker.

"Just bread and some beef, with a measure of rum," Sam confirms. "That, and this here seat by your fire will suit me."

"And what brings you here, my friend? Apart from my excellent beef and the cold outside, that is. I don't recall seeing you here before today."

"I was hoping to find a friend of mine in here. A young lad called Tally."

"Well, if you find him, tell him *I* want to see him. He owes me for the last meal he had, and he's run away on more than one occasion with that fellow Kenny Hawker."

"Kenny Hawker? Isn't he your son?"

"Is he? Well if he is he can still pay me for *his* last meal too. The pair of them are no less than a blessed nuisance, whoever they are."

"Right. I'll keep an eye out for *him* as well."

And as Sam sits down with his rum, awaiting the food, who should walk in through the door but Tally and Hawkes.

SHOOTING THE BRIDGE

"Well, father, how about cheese and beer for the two of us?"

"Of course, Kenny. What father would deny his son and his friend good vittles. Shall I put this on your account as usual?"

"Of course father."

They pick up their filled mugs from the counter and look around for seats. Sam, overhearing the conversation between Hawkes and his father, shakes his head, bemused.

"Here, lad," Sam beckons to Tally, "sit with *me* if you will."

And so the three are sat by the fire, all set to eat.

"I'm surprised to see you up here by London Wall, Sam Bridgewater," says Talman. "I thought that your watering troughs were down Queenhythe way."

"They are indeed, Tally. But you'd be surprised where I might turn up. I'm a Londoner and I feel London deserves the sharing out of my company."

Their food arrives, served by a one armed limping man who somehow is balancing three trenchers along the length of his one remaining arm. He looks at Sam, eyes beseeching him to take his platter of beef for want of ability to offload it. He then turns to Tally for similar assistance with his board of bread and cheese. Next, he hands Hawkes his platter then delves into the pocket of his apron producing a clenched fist of three sharp knives and sets them down one by one in front of each of the three customers. He looks in vain for a gratuitous coin, but to no avail and limps off disgruntled.

"So this is your friend Hawkes, is it?" surmises Sam,

making his own introduction.

"It is, Sam."

"Ah, Kenny. I was speaking with your father just now and he was telling me what a good son you are," suggests Sam, probing for an easy way into conversation.

Hawkes looks at Sam shiftily and say nothing.

"I don't think so, Sam," says Tally. "Jed Hawker doesn't give out such compliments to his son, does he Hawkes?"

"No. At times these days he doesn't even know who I am."

"But do *you* know who you are, my lad? That's the important thing."

Kenworthy Hawker, shuffles uneasy in his chair and stuffs a mouthful of bread and cheese to avoid answering. The truth is, this question sits awkward on him, for he's not one to consider his own actions or demeanour in most things.

"Now then, Tally, let's cut to the chase. I'm not here by chance, as you may perceive. In truth, I'm here to have a word with the two of you… a word concerning your encounter with someone called Jebila."

At the mention of the name, Hawkes looks around furtive for listening ears and chokes on his mouthful of cheese. Coughing to recover, he takes a swig of his beer.

"Sam. Please… be careful," Tally implores the boatman. "I hadn't thought that my mother would tell you of such things. *We've* been sworn to secrecy and I fear for my neck if this is broadcast."

"Well, there you have it. Tell one person and you tell the world. In fact I learned your tale from Goodwife Robson, though your mother added to the story, concerned for her son."

"These things are best left un-talked of, Mister Bridgewater. For our sake and for the sake of all," says Hawkes.

"You're probably right. But my interest is sparked by the origins of this Jebila. You see my own father served in the navy for a spell and on occasion was landed at Tangier when the Portuguese held it. I'm keen to find out more about the place," Sam says all this, cautious against explaining his true purpose for questing information.

"Well, she could often be seen, passing like a whisper, at The Fountain over in Fleet Street," says Tally, opening up to Sam's probing, "but we've not seen her there since our close encounter. Perhaps she fears that her secret is insecure. Look, Sam if you find her you mustn't tell her that I gave you information. Her blade looked sharp as a razor."

"Perhaps she's right to strengthen her disguise with new routines. But I can assure you that, should I find the woman, I'll be as discreet as may be. Now, where exactly is that dismal coffee-house that you told of. Down by the Fleet Ditch, didn't you say?"

Tally explains its whereabouts and Sam, finishing his beef and rum, bids them good day and heads back for Cornhill and Queenhythe.

"What do you think you're doing, Tally, telling him all that?" complains Hawkes. "Who knows *what* that woman will do if she finds out?"

"But, Hawkes, surely, *you're* the one who says you thrive on adventure. And if she tracks us down, I'm sure you'll defend me."

A Fair Frost for a Frost Fair

They order more beer and laugh away the remainder of the morning, forgetful of all things sinister.

The next day, Sam makes his way along Thames Street and close by Puddle Dock crosses into Bristol Street then onwards through several insalubrious alleys until he comes upon the Fleet Ditch. He braves a makeshift bridge to cross the ditch opposite the Bridewell... an austere place governed as it is by Bedlam. And there at the head of the alley that Talman had described to him stands the Turk's Head Coffee-house. The black cat scoots out of the open door and down the gloom-ridden alley as Sam approaches.

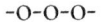

-o-o-o-

4

Jebila

Sam Bridgewater contemplates the strange little carved sign that marks the Turk's Head Coffee-house by the Fleet Ditch, the cat now departed the scene. He enters.

"Can I help you with your needs, kind sir?" comes a greasy, disembodied greeting.

And following close upon the voice, from the darker depths of the ill-lit room, the coffee-house owner appears.

"Coffee would be welcome, if this is indeed the coffee-house advertised by your sign," says Sam, cautious at the unwholesome fellow.

"No one ever comes in here just for coffee, my friend."

"Then what else do you have to offer?" counters Sam, suspicious of the uncouth shopkeeper.

"That depends on what you are prepared to pay."

"Very little. Perhaps the price of coffee."

The oily-looking character, no more than five-feet-three in height and hitherto with every impression of lethargy, quick as lightening stamps on a scurrying cockroach. Sam shudders, more at the disquieting man that at the roach.

"Then coffee is all you'll get."

Jebila

"Certainly it seems I'll not have the company of fellow customers. This place seems far from popular."

"It's early, my friend. Soon this place will be jumping."

"With cockroaches?"

"No... with all the peoples of the world. They all come here as a refuge from the prejudices of this city."

"Then I may be in luck. I'm seeking a woman..."

"Well, you are not alone in that."

"*I* seek a woman from African climes. Yet she is difficult to find for she flits like a butterfly. She wears a mask... a plague-mask," explains Sam

"There *is* such a woman, though I do not know her name. She finds her lodging close by here, the fourth door along the alley, on this side. She is more often there in the daylight hours by all accounts."

"You deserve my thanks," says Sam, "and at least the price of coffee."

As Sam stands to leave he drops coins on the table. The greasy fellow picks up the coins, half smiling and half grimacing on realizing that after all he's sold the information cheaply.

"Good day my friend," offers Sam as he leaves the coffee-house to its bleak promise of customers.

The alley fills Sam with more foreboding as he delves its depths, counting the doors in the murk thrown over the alley by the jettied upper stories.

'One... two...' he counts to himself. Unexpectedly, the black cat jumps down with a squeal from a high windowsill and scurrying under Sam's feet, bolts back up the alley.

"What the...!" Sam calls out aloud in surprise. '*Three...*

SHOOTING THE BRIDGE

four... this must be it.'

The fourth door, dark oak, long-stained from the London weather, moss-ridden at its foot, suggests hidden mysteries. Sam knocks with trepidation. No response. He knocks again, louder now and with purpose. Presently, he hears the bolts shoot and the latch lifts. The door creaks slowly open to a crack no wider than a fist. He perceives a figure peering cautiously... a masked figure, and he catches the brief glint of a blade held defensively across the cloaked chest of a masked woman. It is no plague-mask but simply disguises the eyes. He draws a deep breath.

"Jebila?"

The door slams shut.

He knocks afresh calling: "Please... do not worry. I mean no harm. I simply wish to speak with you concerning a friend... a friend of mine... I believe you know him... Tally Smithson. And *my* name is Samuel Bridgewater, a humble waterman."

The door creaks open once more, wider this time, the blade still held in readiness.

"Step in. Swiftly if you will," she says, darting glances up and down the alley. "The world is always watching."

Sam slips inside, eyes sharp on the dagger. She slams the door shut behind them and bolts it.

"You have no need of the blade, my dear woman, I assure you."

"And how might *you* know *my* needs, stranger? They may be deeper than you think."

"But fear of me should not be among them. Truly, you have no need of the blade."

"Then, I'll trust to your word. But if you prove my trust wrong, you'll regret it sorely. What is your business? Has this Talman friend of yours been telling secrets? I warned him against it."

"He *has*, but through desperation. I assure you he means no ill."

"Yet, he mixes company with Hawkes and, to my knowledge *he* wishes no one well."

"That's as may be, but I have no true interest in Hawkes or his wayward behaviour. Tally is the son of a friend of mine and he has been sorely wronged. He has been deprived of his father, a goldsmith. You may have heard… a pointless murder, down in Cornhill."

"I heard. But you cannot think that I am the murderer?" she protests.

"No, but your conversation with my friend and Hawkes suggests you may be able to help bring the culprit to some justice. You seem to have some knowledge of French slavers and their boats and it's more than possible that there's a link to the dealings of the goldsmith."

"Then if this is true, your quest may well be married to my hidden anger. I have steered well away from all that grief these last months, but to seek redress from the evil slaver?… that might prove most agreeable, and anything I may give to assist it would be given with satisfaction."

-o-o-o-

5

Botolph Wharf

Before anyone knows it, things are getting back to normal on the Thames after the deep frost. The boats are out again yet, now that trade is returning, the bridge seems clogged as ever to overflowing with horses and carts and carriages and people, all jostling to north and to south. And all the revellers and the grumblers are going back to their business, honourable or otherwise.

"Father! Father!" calls out John as he slides his last slide to the foot of Queenhythe Stairs. Will it be the same next year?"

"I hope not lad, unless it's for a very short while. We've work to get back to, the both of us now that you're good for rowing with me every day."

"I know father. I *do* like rowing, and sailing too. And I'll soon be as strong as you. The only thing is, I wish Ellie could have come onto the ice with us. I'm sad that Hannah wouldn't let her join us."

"Well, it's for the best, Johnny. Her mother is a sensible woman and intends to bring up Ellie in proper manner, like a lady. It's enough that you see her at her home for

Botolph Wharf

now, until you're both older... then maybe you can take her onto the river, or perhaps to much more exciting entertainments. Be patient lad. Life's not for rushing unless it be necessary."

The early evening is cold and drab under a grey sky.

"Well met, Sam Bridgewater," Jebila calls cautiously from a shadowy doorway just down from The King's Head off Pudding Lane.

They've arranged to meet here, close by Botolph Wharf. The plague-runner has dispensed with her mask, for now she needs to be discrete rather than so secretive, and a mask would only draw unnecessary attention to her by the waterfront.

"Good day to you, Jebila. Well met indeed. It may be that we can uncover some unwholesome secrets down by the river if we can find your trader."

"Trader. Slaver. Call him what you will. In truth, I have no real desire to find him again but if through you I can help to bring him up sharp, then I'm willing to point you where you may need to go. But be warned, Sam Bridgewater, I shall not be crossed and I shall not be found out. I will disappear like the mist into thin air if there is skulduggery abroad."

"Then we needs must proceed with great care, for both our sakes," agrees Sam. "First let us make way onto Thames Street and on then to the waterside and the Keys beyond the wharf."

"Very well. I'll show you the den of iniquity where that vile French wretch is often seen. It is probable that he and his boat are away gathering other poor souls, indeed I hope they are, for my sake. But you may find more to piece your puzzle even should he be abroad. There are those that deal with him and those that shun him, but all may give you clues as to his trade in gold in this devious city."

"I'd say that there's more chance of that if he *is* away. Absence may make the heart grow fonder, but it makes the tongue grow looser," says Sam.

Making their way along Thames Street, she with the hood of her cloak raised and he with eyes peeled ready for malingerers and cutpurse rogues, they pass Botolph Wharf. On they scurry, by Billingsgate Dock and skirting the Keys until they turn into Great Bear Key not far from the Custom House. Here they come to the very den Jebila had signalled... The Star Inn.

The Keys east of Botolph are unfamiliar to Sam, though the nature of the characters skulking to and fro is all too familiar. They all appear to have some urgent errand, yet they prowl the street all day looking for scraps of advantage in the hostile environment of the docks.

The pair enter The Star and, squeezing through the raucous melee, they find a table in a snug corner. The chaos of activity aids their remaining unnoticed. Sam catches the eye of a serving maid and secures ale for himself, Jebila having declined to drink.

"Look," whispers Jebila. "The roguish fellow with the black eyepatch and the scar above is eye. I saw him down here when the boat landed, I swear. I'm sure he's one of our Frenchman's henchboys. He may know the bastard's whereabouts."

Sam catches the fellow's good eye and beckons him

over apprehensively. He responds, waving away his company of rogues, and saunters over to the snug table. Jebila pulls her hood further forward.

"Join us, fellow," suggests Sam. "We're looking for a Pettifer. We believe you know him?"

Sam catches the jug-maid's attention and signals another pint of ale for his dubious catch.

"I know a *Pelletier*," says the scar-faced fellow, shiftily. "What interests you in Pelletier?" if that indeed is who you mean.

"Oh, we may have business with him. He deals in gold, does he not?" probes Sam with a reassuringly soft tone, inviting the fellow to sup.

"It *has* been known. Gold among other things. Though I know no more than that."

Jebila sits quietly behind her hood, one hand on her hidden blade and seething at the mention of 'other things' but thinking it best for Sam to handle the shifty seaman.

"And where might we find him? Will he be over by Covent Garden?" says Sam, swigging his beer, not sure if he's pushing too hard.

"You mean over by Drury Lane?"

"Yes," says Sam, grateful for this crumb of information.

"You won't find him *there*. He's off in warmer climes. His boat is due back but not yet landed," the fellow informs them. "When he's back, I can tell him you're looking for him. Who shall I say?" he offers, looking suspiciously at Sam now, his alcohol fogged brain clearing a little.

"No. Don't fret, my dear man. We shall seek him then. It's of little import. Perhaps we'll find him over Drury

SHOOTING THE BRIDGE

Lane way in time."

And with that, Sam makes to leave, ushering Jebila before him. Scarface looks perturbed now, thinking maybe he's given too much information for none in return, but allows them by unhindered.

"We'll leave you to return to your company," Sam reassures him, and he and his Moroccan companion are away into the darkened night.

"You know, Jebila. I have a feeling our friend Kenworthy Hawker may know more than he is letting on about this fellow and his hideouts," says Sam to Jebila. "After all, he frequents The Fountain and the bad company there *must* know this Pelletier."

"Well, perhaps you have profited a little from our excursion?"

"I do believe so, my dear."

-o-o-o-

6

Long Acre

Two weeks have passed since Sam met Jebila near The Star Inn off Pudding Lane. Along with plying his trade once more on the river with young Johnny, he's been biding his time and keeping his ear to the ground for news of the Frenchman's return. At last he hears that his boat, The Saint-Germain, has docked.

Sam decides that the best ploy is to seek out the trader near Drury Lane, where he would be set apart from his eye-patched fellow and other unsavoury cronies. Now just *where* exactly remains to be determined. Perhaps Jebila would know, and at least he knows where to find *her*.

Close by the Turk's Head Coffee-house Sam counts the doors once more. *'One... two... three... four...'* He knocks upon the long-stained dark oak door and is presently met with the expected flashing eye and flashing blade.

"Oh, it's you, Sam," says Jebila, opening the door now to let him in. "What news?"

"The Saint-Germain is docked, and with it Pelletier. I intend to seek him out on Drury Lane."

SHOOTING THE BRIDGE

"Then it's well you came here first," says she. "I've found his den there with a few cautious enquiries. I haven't yet laid eyes on him, but now you are here, perhaps it's time to hunt him out."

I've looked for that sly fellow Hawkes," Sam confides, "but he seems to have gone to ground of late. Even Tally Smithson can't, or won't, reveal his whereabouts. No word of him at The *Loon*. Maybe The Fountain is the place."

"We could try, but I've not seen him there either these past weeks."

"Well, let's try Drury Lane and Pelletier first."

"Very well. I'd vowed never to confront him, but mayhap the time has come for it."

The pair of them tread the line of Drury Lane, she plague-masked again, and turn into Long Acre.

"Here, this one," points out Jebila. "Take care, Sam. He's a vile fellow," she adds, fingering the dagger under her cloak.

"I'm more than ready," Sam answers, and knocks boldly on the door.

They hear the creak of boards. The door bolt shoots and the door opens on protesting hinges to reveal a portly fellow, unshaven, but dressed well in expensive cloth and sporting a heavy gold ring.

"And who might *you* be? And on what business?" he asks in halting English and eyeing Jebila with suspicion.

"Good day, Master Pelletier. I am Samuel Bridgewater," answers Sam, endeavouring to sound business-like. "I believe you deal in coins?"

"And if I do, what matter is it to you? And who is your

companion here?"

"It is *I*, master slaver. Do you remember me?" says Jebila,

"I have no idea *who* you are, madam. And perhaps I *now* have no wish to know."

"Well, know you shall," she insists, removing her mask, unable to contain herself, now confronting the despicable man who shipped her here to England.

"Does Tangier ring in your memory? Jebila was my home, and Jebila is my name."

"Ah, Tangier. I do recall. A thorny bitch you were and no doubt are," he hisses in recognition, recoiling to a safer distance in his hallway. "You both had better come in off the street if it's business you intend. And as for you madam, if you will forgive me, you surely have found a better life here than in that godforsaken place. There is no need for animosity."

"I had a life in Tangier and *you* stole it. For that alone I hold a grudge, monsieur. As for Sam's business, I withhold my disdain for you in deference to him."

"Very well, I am always open for business… at the right price."

"Then let us hope the price is not too great," says Sam. "There are two particular coins I have an interest in."

With this, Sam is bold enough to tell the story of Zeke Smithson's demise and the loss of the coins, and in doing so careful not to point the finger at the trader.

"I have sold many a coin to many a goldsmith, Samuel Bridgewater. There is no crime in that, I trust. And, yes, I *do* remember those coins… they were very special. Very rare. But I can assure you, I would have no wish to sell them twice over," he insists, perceiving the cloaked inference behind Sam's tale of murder. "I received a fair price for them from this Zeke as you call him. I cannot see that we have any business to conduct here."

"So say you, but we may yet have further need. Tell me, do you have dealings with Kenworthy Hawker?"

"Hawkes?" laughs Pelletier. "That insufferable rogue? Does anyone have true dealings with him? I would rather cut my own hand off than shake his."

"Then perhaps we need to deal with him further ourselves, for the time being. But be warned, if I find that you have aught to do with him or with Zeke's demise, you will rue the day."

Jebila hisses in agreement and the pair turn to leave without a further word.

As they step into the street, Pelletier calls after them.

"Good riddance, sir. I can do no business with the likes of you, I fear. And, madam, be grateful that you are in this civilised place."

Jebila turns with a chilling growl, drawing her blade as the trader slams shut his door.

"Let it be, Jebila. I have business with Hawkes, I think. There is a link, I'm sure of it. I'll speak with Talman Smithson. He is sure to tell his whereabouts, if pushed. I'll call on you again, when I have intelligence of the matter, assuming that you are as keen as me to fathom the dire tragedy of the Smithsons."

"You intrigue me, Sam Bridgewater. I never met a man so honourable and yet more determined. I think you have an easy spot for this Hannah."

"Let's say it's just so tragic, the circumstances she finds

herself in, and I have sympathy with that."

"We all be tragic, friend Sam. Unless we be oblivious fools."

"I fear you are right, Jebila, my dear."

"So where's the best place for me to find your good friend Hawker these days, Talman?" asks Sam.

"I'm sorry, Samuel. I haven't seen Hawkes for a while now. I fear he's too deep for me."

"You're best keeping clear of him. He's a bad piece of work if my nose is keen as ever it was."

"What did I tell you, Talman?" says Hannah.

"Mother, I can look after myself. I know when company is best parted with."

"Perhaps you are learning then, for I'm unsure it was ever thus."

"So you haven't visited The Fountain recently, Talman?" asks Sam.

"No. Nor Rainbow's," Tally replies, sheepishly.

"And The Man in the Moon?"

"No. I've not seen Hawkes or his loon of a father."

Sam's keen nose twitches with a feeling that Tally is not entirely forthcoming regarding Kenworthy Hawker.

"Then I needs must find him myself. Perhaps they'll have wind of him at The Fountain or at Rainbow's, or maybe Jed Hawker will ken where he might be found."

-o-o-o-

7

Hawker's Moon

Sam calls on Jebila once more and when they reach The Fountain Inn they find it, as is its custom, to be full of reprobates who do not work at a living and whores who do. But there is no sign of Hawkes and by all accounts he's not been there for a fair while.

"No. Can't say I've seen him in weeks, and his slate is far from clean," says the landlord. "No sign of his sorry companion either... Tally isn't it?"

"It is," says Sam.

"You won't find that little weasel Hawkes here," shouts a heavily painted strumpet in a crimson gown, all cerise, coloured lips and cleavage. "Last time he ruffled *my* feathers he was away without a by-your-leave or the sniff of a purse. If you find 'im, kick 'im in the balls for me, will you?"

"Then you think he's shy of returning to meet your wrath," suggests Sam.

"Too right you are, darlin'. If I get my hands on 'im it's more than wrath he'll meet, useless bugger that he is."

Sam and Jebila leave her to her anger and find the

street.

"I have a mind to try Rainbow's," says Sam.

"It's not likely he'd come so close to The Fountain if Red Rosie's outburst is anything of a guide."

"Even so, it's there we go and if that is a fool's errand then maybe The *Loon* in the Moon should cast some light."

There's no news of him to be had at Rainbow's, so the pair head back east for Hawker's Moon.

At The *Loon*, all is subdued, until Jed Hawker gets excited, lamenting the price of beef, bending the ear of a reluctant customer.

"How can I hold the price of an ordinary, when the meat becomes ever more costly?"

"I can't be bothered with that, Jed," says the would be diner. My purse is a fair bit leaner than *your* beef. How do think I'm to manage to the end of the week?"

"You'll just have to live on turnips, Nickerson, you old bugger. They're ripening on the tree out back as we speak."

"You ain't got no turnip tree out there, Jed Hawker."

"What? Who's stolen it? I won't have it, I won't."

"Well, nor will *I*, since you ain't got any. I'd better cough up for the beef then. And I hope the bread's fresh."

"Give it a rest, Nickerson, you sot," calls Hawkes who's sat with his booted feet on a table, half hidden in the shadow of a heavy curtain near the fire mantle.

"Sot? *You're* the sot, Kenny Hawker… always with a pint of sac to hand. I don't know what you were thinking, Jed when you brought *him* into the world."

"It weren't me that did that. It were his mother. She

were the daft bugger that got herself pregnant. She were too easy in them days, but you couldn't get a slice of ham between her thighs now, let alone a sausage."

"Leave it out, dad," interrupts Hawkes.

"I ain't got no choice," Jed replies.

"And that's good is it?" asks Nickerson.

"It is… if you don't want another Kenny Hawker, it is."

Sam and Jebila step into the eating house on the tail end of this strange conversation. They're about to interrupt Jed to ask the whereabouts of the elusive Hawkes, when they spy him wrapped in the shadow of his curtain.

"Ah, just the fellow," Sam calls out, in feigned pleasure at the sight of the insalubrious idler. He snatches a tanker of ale and makes his way over.

Jebila sidles in between them, trying to remain inconspicuous to the other customers.

"You're an elusive fellow these days, Master Hawker. You seem to have gone to ground. You certainly seem to have dropped our friend Tally Smithson like a stone. Has someone clipped your wings?"

"What business is it of yours, Sam Bridgewater?"

"Well, I'll tell you what business I have. I think you know a thing or two about an acquaintance of mine… Trader Pelletier's his name."

At the mention of the name, Jebila thumps the table in pent up irritation and Hawkes startles, but Sam's not sure if it's for fear of the name or of Jebila.

"I've never heard the name," counters Hawkes.

"Well, he tells us *he* knows *you*."

Another thump of the table from the masker: "You seem happy enough to spread word of people when it suits you, so why not now?"

"I told you, I don't know this Pelletier. And anyway, I'm expecting a business acquaintance any minute now, so I can spare you no more idle chat."

"Well, then young Hawkes. Be warned. If I find that you know more than you're admitting, I'll be on you tail."

And with that, he and Jebila make to leave. As they reach the door, who should be entering this *Loon* of a meeting place other than Kaleb Tasker, the goldsmith. He casts a shifty eye at Sam and his unlikely companion as he brushes by on his way to Hawkes' table.

In the street, Sam says to Jebila: "Be away for now, my dear. I have a further appointment with master Hawkes and this unexpected business fellow."

"Take care then, Sam. They're a rum pair."

"Don't worry. The back door and a curtain will aid me in eavesdropping."

Sam heads back in and secretes himself within easy earshot of the pair.

"So, Hawker. we meet at last," says Tasker, glancing around to ensure no one is near. "You are hard to find."

"Well, I prefer to keep a quiet counsel these days. There are odd things afoot since the death of your fellow, the goldsmith. I don't know why the fuss. There are people dispatched every day in this hell hole of a city."

"You may say so, but the death of a goldsmith is not so readily missed. You'll recall a while ago, a peruke was found below Queenhythe near the bridge. Turns out he was a renowned member of The Company of Barbers and Surgeons, cut with his own blades rumour has it. There are people who pay attention, for the guilds all are thick as thieves, and much fuss was made of it at first. And yet the constables are not up to the job, I fear. The cutter *may* be tracked down and justice meted out, but you can never be sure of it. Yet, when they find a beggar's cap, or even its occupant, no one gives a damn anyway. Now with Zeke Smithson, people *are* paying a degree of attention but all for naught is my guess. For myself, I didn't like the man overmuch. He did me no favours in business, and I returned the compliment. I wouldn't wish him dead *myself*, but there are those who would. Good riddance is in the minds of some."

"Well, as you will be aware, I know the family, and I can see little harm in them. Tally, the goldsmith's son, has been a companion, though he's a watery fellow. I don't see him these days."

"But are you hiding from others than him? I shouldn't wonder, with *your* reputation that you might be tied in with all this intrigue."

"No more than *you* might be, Tasker. Your dire reputation is not earned for nothing."

"You may say so, but I know my business and ruthless we sometimes need to be."

"So, to the point, Tasker. What business do you wish with me?"

"Well, there is one of our company that I really *cannot* abide. You may have heard the name of James Otway. He has taken sides with Hannah Smithson, always casting me in a bad light, though I imagine I have been the maker of my own misfortune with her. I knew of your friendship with her son and had thought you might, through him, cast a better light on me for the benefit of his mother and to the detriment of Otway. But if you are distant from him now, I'm on a fool's errand, I fear, at any price, though it might be worth a coin or two to your pocket."

"Perhaps not at any price, Tasker. I will think over your proposition and let you know when I've had time to reflect."

And with that, Kaleb Tasker stood to leave.

"Then I'll catch up with you again, very soon," says Tasker.

"Perhaps," replies Hawkes.

And Tasker is gone. Sam sneaks out the way he came in, pondering on Hawker and Tasker and the intrigue that was spoken between them.

'Perhaps there is something in their conversation that points to Zeke Smithson's murder."

When Woodcock Skeleton takes up a second pint of ale at The Lion Inn in Birdcage Alley in Southwark he's surprised to see Kenworthy Hawker walk in.

"Hawkes, you fickle fellow. What brings *you* to Southwark on such a fine afternoon?"

"I'm looking for your advice, Woodcock. There's a certain rogue that I may have business with and I'm hoping for intelligence on the man."

"Now, I'm more used to dealing with *uncertain* rogues... such as yourself, Hawkes. But a *certain* one makes for interesting fare."

"I'm talking of a goldsmith called Tasker. He wants me to promote his good character with a lady I know."

"Tasker?" now there's a name I know. I've had vague dealings with him and a few others of that *Worshipful*

Company; Fletcher, Otway, Harrington... all rogues in their own way. And I heard of the fate of Hezekiah Smithson... I gather he dealt with Pelletier, the French slaver for his sins."

"But is Tasker worthy of praise to this good woman?"

"How should *I* know? I've only met with him twice. Then again, why should I care? Do it, boy. It'll do you no harm, and maybe some good. But get paid in advance, and if you keep your eye in, you may pick up a subtle trinket or two which I'd be happy to share with you. In fact you could do worse than ease you way of a dark night into any of those goldsmiths' premises, for they all have rich pickings poorly guarded truth be known. Fletcher keeps his baubles in an old and battered trunk I hear, and Otway, one of the richest, pays little regard to *his* security so I'm told. And remember... you owe me, after all, for those earlier favours, Hawkes."

"I've not forgotten it, Woodcock. How could I?"

"So true, for I will not *let* you forget it until the debt is paid."

"My dearest John, how pleasant to see you," says Hannah Smithson, greeting the boy who has turned up presenting a neatly wrapped parcel.

"This is from father, Missus Smithson. He's very busy on the river and so could not get along to see you himself these next few days. He says that if it were summertime, he would send you flowers, but in their stead that these would cheer you in the cold of winter. Please missus, Is Ellie at home?"

"She *is*, my dear. She's in our little garden, attending to weeds and such. She will be glad to see you. Go on through now. And John, please call me Hannah, if you will. As I've told you before... not so formal, Johnny."

Hannah prises open the delicate little parcel to find a pair of elegantly sown gloves.

"My, oh my," she sighs wistfully. "Just the sort of gift that Zeke would bring me. How shall I ever forget?"

"Hello, John," greets Ellie, as the boy steps out into the garden. "How nice that you've come."

"I came to bring a gift from father to your mother, but truly, I came to see you with a gift of my own," he says, thrusting a little packet wrapped in a fragment of sailcloth into her tiny hand.

"What is it? What is it?" she says excitedly, tearing at the cloth.

He lets her open the little prize without replying.

"Oh, it's lovely. What A beautiful brooch. Where did you buy it?"

"I didn't. I found it down by the riverside. When the Frost Fair was here. I've been keeping it saved for you."

"Oh dear. Then someone has lost it. I'm sure they will be very sad to lose such a beautiful thing."

"Perhaps, but they should have guarded it more carefully. I do hope that *you* will treasure it?"

"Oh, I will, dear Johnny. Always."

"This is such a lovely little garden, Ellie."

"Yes. I help mother to keep it tidy. You should see it in the springtime. The blossoms are full of *such* colour."

"Father says that my mother loved flowers, but they came, when she could afford them, from the market at Covent Garden," the boy says, pensively.

"Do you miss her, Johnny?"

"I do, though I don't really remember her. She was gone before I was four years old. Do *you* miss your father, Ellie?"

"Yes, I miss him every day. So does mother. I think she sometimes cries, but tries not to let me see her sadness," replies Ellie, wiping a forming tear from her eye.

"When I grow up, I'm going to be rich and have a really big and beautiful garden with lots of bright flowers," says John, trying to cheer her.

"And I will visit you there, John, I promise."

"Of course you will. I shall need someone to tend the weeds, of course."

"But if you're rich, we shall... I mean *you* shall have a gardener."

Hannah is placing her delightful new gloves with care in a drawer when there is a knock on the door. She turns the latch to discover that James Otway is stood on the step, stamping his feet from the cold.

"I'm so sorry to arrive unannounced, my dear, but wished to see how you are faring in you sad circumstance. You did not attend our recent meeting of The Company and I feared it may be through melancholy."

"No, my dear Mister Otway. I am sad of course. I *did* intend to come to the meeting but I have my own business to mind, which is both fair and my own," she says, trying at once to discourage the man, yet to remain polite.

"But I know how lonely life can be, dearest Hannah," he persists. "Surely I could visit you on a regular basis? It need not *all* be about business."

"I do appreciate your concerns, Mister Otway, but I fear you are in danger of overstepping the mark. Perhaps you should pay more attention to your relationship with Mister Tasker. He seems in need of some consolation in life... far more than I."

"Very well, Hannah. I do understand your reticence in this. Perhaps at some later date we may discuss such things further."

"Perhaps," she says politely, not wishing to indulge him.

She shows him to the door and is rescued from further discourse on the step with the goldsmith by the arrival of her son, Talman.

"And what business did Mister Otway have here, mother?" asks Talman, latching the door behind the departing visitor.

"Oh, something and nothing, my boy," she says dismissively. "He is a nice enough fellow and well-meaning I'm sure, but rather forward in his advances of assistance and in concern for my wellbeing."

"You would be far better showing a kind face to Kaleb Tasker, mother. I have it on good authority that he is a reliable and sincere man."

"Good God, Talman. Who on earth would tell you that? The man is an obnoxious mountebank deserving nothing but contempt."

"It was Hawkes who told me. He says he's had many a dealing with Tasker and that he's always proved true to his word."

"Hawkes? If you believe Kenny Hawker in anything, you are in need of a doctor. Any quack would tell you that

SHOOTING THE BRIDGE

your mind is out of kilter."

"Well, that's what Hawkes *said*. Whilst I've been out of touch with him of late, I met him at The *Loon* yesterday and I still value his opinion."

"The *Loon*... an appropriate place... for both of you I fear. I'll hear no more of it."

At that moment, Ellie and John come in from the garden.

"I'm away home now, Missus Smith... Missus Hannah. I have to meet with father on the riverside to help this afternoon," says John.

"Mother," calls out Ellie, holding out her open hand, "look at this beautiful present Johnny has brought for me. I shall treasure it always."

"Yes, dear Ellie. It is very beautiful and well-given. You must always treasure gifts when they are true-intended but also be wary, for some men give gifts with *false* intentions, as indeed do some women. You still have so much to learn, my love."

Johnny bids farewell and runs to the street, wondering if he really has true or false intentions.

-o-o-o-

8

Gold for the Taking

It's a grim night in Southwark, all river mist and threatening frost. Kenworthy Hawker is on an errand to see his mentor in crime, Snakehead Skeleton. The damp reek of Birdcage Alley, lit only by a passing linkboy's light and a lone lanthorn hung in the porch of an inn, is clinging to him and like a sponge his greatcoat is soaking up the murk. His very bones shudder and he shivers as he enters The Lion Inn.

"Woodcock? Where is Woodcock?" asks Kenworthy excitedly.

"In the back room, my friend," says the landlord. "He has a sore head like a bear this night. If I were you, I'd go carefully."

Hawkes clutches his leather carry-bag closer to him and slips to the back room, opening the door to a crack and cautiously peeking in.

"Woodcock?" he whispers, gingerly. "It's me, Hawkes."

"What in the Devil's name do *you* want?" Skeleton snaps. "You should be tucked in bed with your pillows and blankets on a night like this."

"I've brought treasure. At great peril, I might add. You were right about Otway. It was an easy task. I just grabbed handfuls of stuff and I've left no trace. Though all hell will break out in the morning is my guess... when he wakes and finds out that his precious bounty has been diminished."

"I see," says Skeleton, perking from his pique. "So what do you have for *me*?"

"Now," says Hawkes, as he delves into his bag. "I give you this in full settlement of my debt to your favours. Right?"

"Let me see first and I'll be the judge of your compensation."

Hawkes lays down a gold amulet and several coins upon the beer-swilled table.

"Mmh? You could maybe have done better, but I suppose it's all I could expect from the likes of *you*, Hawkes. Fair due. We'll call it quits. But you can buy me a pint of ale to sign it off."

Hawkes slinks off to the bar like an obedient dog, clutching his bag with its depleted contents.

-o-o-o-

9

Tower Wharf

"Your boat, my man, if you please. I have pressing need to cross the river."

"Pressing is it, Tally Smithson?" says Sam Bridgewater. "Time is only pressing if we make it so, I fear. And I fear you make it so all too often."

"Oh, it's *you*, Sam," says Talman Smithson in surprise. "I had no idea your boat was so impressive. I'd thought it a mere rowboat, but your sail will add to our speed. And if I choose to make time urgent, then that is my affair and you of all folk should be mindful of the needs of others. I must be in Southwark with some urgency."

"I'd understood that your usual need for haste these days is to get to the alehouse or mayhap to The Duke's Theatre over in Dorset Gardens. In fact I'm surprised you've never stepped onto my boat before now to give you passage to that house of deception."

"I prefer to stay on land whenever I can. The water gives me the shakes."

"*I* hear you've been taking to the stronger stuff lately. I'd have thought that would shake you more."

SHOOTING THE BRIDGE

"It seems my routines are more a matter for your interest than they should be, Sam Bridgewater. I suppose all this tittle-tattle comes from my mother."

"Well, if it does, I'm sure she has your best interests at heart. You should trust to her judgement more than you appear to do. She's a good and sensible woman."

"Look. It's your *own* watery business you should be minding. And right now *I* have watery business for you, so please put your mind to it, if you will."

"Then hand your bag to Johnny. He'll stow it safe for you."

"I can manage it well enough myself, thanks."

"Then step steady and mind the rock of the boat."

Ignoring the good advice, the young hothead jumps onto the rear seat-plank, almost toppling himself and the boatmen into the dark waters of the Thames. Sam steadies the boat with the skill of years and Talman crams the bag he's carrying behind the seat.

"Sit down, you lumbering idiot, Talman," shouts Sam. "You'll have us all overboard together."

Tally sits admonished, yet preoccupied. Sam pushes off from Queenhythe Stairs and Johnny hoists the sail deftly catching the downstream westerly breeze.

"I'll ask no more of your business, young Talman. But I trust you have good purpose in your errand. Southwark smacks of mischief more oft than not, but some do good there, I suppose."

"Well do-gooders should do their own good deeds and leave others to do *theirs*."

"Very well, though I sometimes fear for your wellbeing, more for your mother's sake than for your own. But I'll do your bidding and trust what common sense you have will steer you right. You needn't dig for coins."

It's mid-afternoon and the day is bright and clear. Old Man Thames is in fair spate on an outgoing tide, but Sam is master of the conditions and with John to help they are a good team. The three sit in silence for the crossing and, negotiating the other vessels plying their river-trade, Sam brings the boat into safe mooring on the south bank, Johnny stows the sail and Talman, retrieving his bag, makes to alight onto the quayside baulks.

"Well, well, well. If it isn't friend Tally," says a familiar voice from the walkway above them. "Now *there's* a coincidence, if ever there was one," says Kenworthy Hawker. "Me and Skeleton here were on our way to see you, weren't we, Woodcock? I thought you may have something of mine."

"We were indeed, Hawkes," concurs Woodcock Skeleton, jumping uninvited into the boat, drawing a knife and pointing its lethal tip at Tally.

Tally shrinks back down to the seat, cowering behind the bag now.

"Take care, you crazy fool. You'll upend us," protests Sam, at the same time wondering what is to ensue.

"No need for knives, Woodcock," says Hawkes. "Tally is a true friend, aren't you Tally?"

"Of course, Hawkes. *I* was on my way to see *you*... at The Lion," says Tally. "Your father said I'd catch you there. And I've brought your bag, Hawkes. You were a fool to leave it at The *Loon*. It could so easily have been stolen."

"Happen you're right, but I was trusting you would

SHOOTING THE BRIDGE

have picked it up," says Hawkes grabbing the bag. "You haven't tampered with it, have you? If so, I won't answer for my wrath, Tally, dear friend."

"How could you doubt me, Hawkes. As you say, you know I am a true and honest friend. How *could* you doubt me?"

"We're not a little suspicious of most anyone in this godforsaken city, Tally," says Hawkes, speaking as if he were apprenticed to Snakehead Skeleton. "I'm sorry for mistrusting you," he adds, dubiously.

"Look you. Time and the river wait for no man," scolds Woodcock Skeleton. "Now Hawkes here has his bag and its contents, we're urgent to meet our associate, Mr. Otway. So, master boatman... you can turn this hulk around and take us all back across the river," declares Skeleton menacingly. He turns the attention of his blade to young John.

'James Otway?' thinks Sam. 'What business would these two have with him, I wonder?'

Hawkes jumps aboard and sits on the plank, sidling up to Tally and grabbing his bag. Tally winces.

"You seem to presume you are master of proceedings, Mister Woodcock," ventures Tally.

"You bloody fool, Tally," murmurs Hawkes behind a raised hand. You don't know half of what he can be like."

"Sometimes I really don't know why I've hung with you, Hawkes," says Tally, on the point of weeping. "Perhaps my mother is right. I should stay away from the likes of you and your company," he whispers, so as not to anger Skeleton.

"Hung with me... that's a possibility, dear Tally. And

it's too late for denouncing me, my friend. You should have thought of your mother before now, if you owe her your allegiance. I thought you were with me all the way, but you're clearly unclear in your purpose in life."

"Hush your mumblings, you two," shouts Skeleton, rocking the boat once more and sitting down next to Johnny, the five of them now filling it almost to the rowlocks. "We have serious business to do. And sharp about it, back to Queenhythe, master boatman, or it'll be worse for your boy here."

Sam grits his teeth, powerless in the face of the threat. There's something familiar about this loathsome oaf. And then he sees it… the tattoo upon the left side of his neck, peeking out from that same grimy neckerchief… the repulsive snake's head.

The boatman pushes off into the mainstream of the river. Johnny instinctively raises the sail, despite the threat of Skeleton's blade. Sam's at the tiller, his mind racing, trusting that once they reach the haven of the north bank these three madmen can do what they will, providing he and his son are left unscathed. His concentration gone for a moment, they narrowly avoid collision with a rowboat battling west against the current. Johnny is skilfully manoeuvring the sail, cajoling the jib to best compensate for the flow, but the near collision puts him off his young stride, the boat now turns all wrong and, seemingly out of nowhere, looms a river barge heading west itself… and their fate is inevitable as they strike a glancing blow at the stern quarters of the barge.

"John! No!" cries out Sam, as the boy is launched over the side into the brooding waters with a loud splash.

SHOOTING THE BRIDGE

Instinctively, Sam turns the boat sharply to the east to run with the flow and over go Skeleton and Hawkes. The three of them, human jetsam, splash and flounder as they're swept towards the fearsome buttresses of London Bridge. John, a swimmer, holds his own as the other two fly by him like twigs on a lively stream, then he too is overpowered by the surging river.

"For God's sake, Talman. Sit tight. We're after them," hollers Sam. "Hold on, John. I'm with you," he shouts to the boy.

The boatman, with all the years of his skill, grapples with the sail ropes but the bridge, with its cruel buttresses, comes up to meet them all... the boat is still twenty yards behind the over-boarders. Skeleton is gasping, clutching at thin air, Hawkes is clambering, frantic and ruthless on top of the raft that is Skeleton. Johnny is still fighting the flow and is the last of the three to be sucked into the shadow of the bridge and spewed out on the other side, bobbing, a hopeful cork.

"Shit!" cries Sam. "...must shoot the bridge."

And with the frantic spume flying into his face, he somehow manages to drop the sail and then the mast. He and Tally in their bullet of a boat fly under the arches on white water and are fired like a musket ball into the nether reaches of the Thames.

"John!" he calls out desperately. "Use the bend in the river. Swim for Tower Wharf."

The boat is gaining on John, but the other two are sweeping on at great speed in the mainstream. Sam can make out Hawkes, still frantic in the water, like a sinking windmill, but Skeleton now submerges out of sight.

Tower Wharf

Talman, until now enthralled by their plight, stiff as a cadaver, of a sudden bursts into action. He grabs an oar, fighting to release it from its rowlock. As they pull alongside a drifting John, he thrusts out the oar offering it like to an olive branch.

"Grab hold, young John," he calls in desperation.

The boy reaches out and misses, spinning and floating onwards. Sam has the mast up and the sail hoisted again and works the boat to Tally's best advantage for another try.

"Again, John," calls out Tally.

John, almost sunk from exhaustion, makes a desperate lunge and grasps the oar with both hands. With all his might, Tally hoists him aboard, the boy spluttering and coughing foul water from exhausted lungs. Sam turns the boat to safe mooring at Tower Wharf. Tally, himself shivering from the wet chaos, removes his coat and drapes it over the shaking boy. With a sigh of relief, Sam looks east and catches the last vestiges of Kenworthy Hawker as he sinks to join Woodcock Skeleton in the deep undercurrents, lost to eternity.

Talman turns and steps back upon the plank he'd been seated on, stumbling over Hawkes' bag as he does so.

-o-o-o-

10

A Goldsmith Too Far

There's a loud rapping on the door of the Smithson's house up on Cornhill.

"My God! Talman!" exclaims Hannah Smithson, as she opens the door to the sight of her son.

He stands there, snivelling and shrivelled like an over-cured wet kipper.

"What on earth..."

"We've had a lucky escape, Hann," Sam assures her as he ushers Tally Smithson inside followed by young Johnny who is brighter by far than the goldsmith's son. "But there's a sorry tale to tell, for sure."

And the waterman relates the story of the calamity that has befallen Kenny Hawker and Woodcock Skeleton.

"The constables have been informed and they're making a token effort at finding the wretches, but they'd have better luck searching the waters at Greenwich by now."

"Quickly, the three of you. Get you around the fire whilst I find you something dry to put on. And look you... Goody Robson's here helping in the kitchen.

A Goldsmith Too Far

There's broth in the pot. It will see you warmed.

"It's not fish broth is it, Hannah?" asks Johnny, plaintively.

"No, John. It's chicken, my dear. Do you not care for fish broth?"

"No, Hannah. It's always *damp*. It's like it's been dragged along in the Thames then boiled afresh. But I *do* like chicken broth."

Sam smiles at his son knowingly, then presents a bundle that he's been holding.

"This is Hawkes' bag, Hannah. Talman was looking to return it to Hawker. The rogue had left it behind at The Man in the Moon when they last met there."

"Then should it not be handed to the constables?" asks Hannah.

"In good time, my dear," says Sam. "You see, we peeked inside, didn't we Talman?"

"Yes, Sam."

"And what did we find there among its treasure? We found two gold coins which, remarkably, look to be the ones that your Hezekiah paid so dearly for. You'll find them in there."

"My Lord!" calls out Hannah. "You mean those two rogues were my poor Zeke's killers."

"It's possible, Hannah, though I think it goes deeper," says Sam. "You see, from what the pair declared before we fell foul of the river, they had business with James Otway. And yet we gathered that it's Otway himself that Hawkes robbed only last week. The bag's contents are surely part of the stash and it may be that they conspired to sell the spoils afresh to him with some concocted tale as

SHOOTING THE BRIDGE

to how they came by them. Yet I suspect they knew not that those particular coins were in the goods stolen. It's more than likely that Otway had some hand in Zeke's killing, I fear?"

"But surely, James Otway is an upstanding member of The Guild, Sam," says Hannah. "He would know that the coins were Zeke's. He would never have traded to buy them."

"Indeed not, if indeed he is upstanding. Yet is seems he *was* in possession of them. It's a merry dance that the coins have been on. And we need to draw the tune to an end. Tally and I shall visit the man and see what he has to say for himself."

"But, surely this is a matter for the constables, Sam?"

"In time, my dear. We would wait until next Christmas if we left it to them, and even then we may expect no epiphany."

"I'm sorry, masters, but I am rather busy with my colleague Tasker here. What business do you have for me today," James Otway says, as he greets Talman and Sam at his door.

"Perhaps we'd best come in to discuss such business as we *do* have," says Sam.

"Very well, but be sure to make it brief, sirs. Time and tide wait for no man and I would suggest that Kaleb here has first call on my time today."

"That's as maybe, Mister Otway," says Talman. "Yet you may find what we have to discuss has some import for you."

Kaleb Tasker stands to one side, wondering what in the world this business can be.

"I believe these may be yours?" suggests Sam, prising two bright coins from the bag which he's brought with him.

"And what makes you think so? I don't believe I've set eyes upon them before. But they look as if they may be the coins that were taken from dear Hezekiah Smithson."

"Indeed, we believe they *are*, my friend. And I believe one Woodcock Skeleton and his enthralled companion Kenworthy Hawker planned to sell their spoils back to you, they having stolen them from you but recently."

Otway, off his guard and feeling cornered by the accusation, irrationally makes to run. Tasker grabs him.

"So, I was right to doubt your probity, James Otway," says Tasker. "You were clearly reluctant to place the matter of the theft from you before the authorities... for fear of them linking you with these two little treasures, no doubt."

"There is nothing to link me with those coins, Kaleb Tasker," retorts Otway.

But the constables are called and Otway is hastily hauled away for interrogation.

Spring 1677. He hears no splash... Sam Bridgewater, waterman on the Thames, sits contemplative, thankful for a quiet afternoon moored off Queenhythe after ferrying three clergymen across to the Southwark side on a calm flow. His son, John, is away visiting his soulmate Eliska at the Smithson's.

'It's good to see the boy happy,' he thinks. *'He works so hard on the water with me, always looking to learn new skills, and not just from the river. He's hungry for knowledge of the world*

SHOOTING THE BRIDGE

around him and puts his learning to good use. I'm sure Hannah regards him with as much pride as I do. And that way a future lies for him, I'm sure of it.'

The weather is set fair and the warmth is in the sun on a good day when the wind is kind. London Bridge sits downstream on benign buttresses today.

Hannah Smithson has made her peace with Kaleb Tasker and he is more conciliatory in his ways, having realized how obnoxious he'd become. Yet it was he who had been on the trail of James Otway ahead of Sam and Jebila. If it were not for the turn of events with Snakehead Skeleton and Kenny Hawkes drowning, Tasker would have endeavoured to bring Otway to book in time. But the constables found no clear evidence of Otway's involvement in the dark deed done to Zeke Smithson. Money sways things in odd directions sometimes and somehow James Otway escaped the heavier hand of the law, heaping all the guilt on the two drowned rogues. And once he was acquitted, he thought better of chancing his future luck in London and is gone to pursue other deceptions further north, in the midlands.

For *his* part, Sam has become much a part of Hannah Smithson's life, and whilst she makes her living in gold, she hankers secretly after a simpler life.

As for Talman? Now *there's* an odd story. With Hawkes dead and gone, Tally is back on the straight and narrow. He no longer visits the likes of Rainbow's Coffee-house, or The Fountain Inn with its iniquitous crew. Instead, he's strengthened his liking for the *Loon*; both the eating house *and* the *Loon* that is Jed Hawker. Jed hardly understands that his son has gone and in his stead has adopted

Talman, in a manner of speaking. And Talman ensures that all the fine vittles he enjoys there are paid for in full and in timely fashion.

Goody Robson continues to do good deeds and to spread the news provided by all and sundry. Unwittingly, she sometimes falls victim of those who wish to spread a malicious word or two aided by her gossiping.

Jebila, enigma that she is, decides that her past encounters with Pelletier are best left to lie where they have fallen. She is pleased to think that she may have helped Sam to solve the mystery of the coins, and whilst she retreats to the backstreets around the Fleet Ditch once more, she occasionally comes across Sam plying his trade west of Queenhythe. She no longer wears her mask.

'All this water under the bridge,' thinks Sam as he stows his boat for the day and heads to Hannah Smithson's to find his son.

"One day," says Hannah to Sam, "times will be different for us all."

"There are true words in that, Hannah," says Sam, knowing that she means for the better, "but will they bring us good fortune, I wonder. Shall we learn our lessons from the past?"

"Well, father," says Johnny. "*I've* learned lots of things. You always *did* tell me that the sneaky ones might be the ones to watch. And that noisy fellow, Kaleb, was the good one, wasn't he. 'Handsome is as handsome does. That's a lesson worth observing,' is what you said."

You're right, young John," answered Sam, with a broad smile. "You're *so* right, my boy."

~FINIS~

Printed in Great Britain
by Amazon